# Chase

# The Blues

# Away

Ivan and Abbie
Summer Lake Seasons Book Four

## By SJ McCoy

A Sweet n Steamy Romance

Published by Xenion, Inc

Copyright © 2019 SJ McCoy

Published by Xenion, Inc.
First paperback edition 2019
www.sjmccoy.com

This book is a work of fiction. Names, characters, places, and events
are figments of the author's imagination, fictitious, or are used
fictitiously. Any resemblance to actual events, locales or persons
living or dead is coincidental.

Cover Design by Dana Lamothe of Designs by Dana
Editor: Mitzi Pummer Carroll
Proofreaders: Aileen Blomberg, Marisa Nichols, Traci Atkinson.

ISBN: 978-1-946220-61-5

# Dedication

*This one is for Abbie*

*It started with a nipple!*

*And I guess I'll leave the rest to the reader's imagination.*

*What I will say is thanks for helping a writer out.*

*And thank you, too, for letting me borrow your name.*

*Love*

*SJ*

*oxo*

# Chapter One

Ivan set the weights back on the rack and rolled his shoulders. He was tired tonight. He'd told himself that he'd finish his workout with a run on the treadmill. It'd been too cold to run outside for over a week now—or at least, that's what he'd kept telling himself. He didn't mind lifting weights; he enjoyed it, but he was too quick to make excuses about getting his cardio in. He looked around as he wiped the bench and the weights down. It was quiet in the gym tonight. It was later than usual, though, too. He smiled to himself. Maybe if he got out of here, Russ would be able to close up early.

He started making his way to the locker room, giving the row of treadmills the side-eye as he went. He could come in on the weekend and do an hour then instead.

His stride faltered when the door to the women's locker room opened. His heart rate, which had been returning to normal, picked right back up at the sight of the woman who came out. It was Abbie! He stopped and smiled as she came closer, but she didn't notice him. She had earbuds in her ears and was looking down, occupied with her phone. She walked by him without lifting her gaze and got on the first treadmill.

Ivan hesitated only a moment before following her. He'd intended to get some cardio in, after all. She was just the motivation he needed. He thought better of getting on the treadmill right beside hers. There was no need to crowd her. He left two empty and got on the fourth one in line. He doubted anyone would come in and get between them.

He started the machine up at a brisk walk and glanced over at her. She turned, and her eyes widened in recognition when she saw him. A shot of adrenaline coursed through his veins as her gaze locked with his. He wanted to smile or say hello or do something—anything—that would count as normal human interaction, but there was nothing normal about that moment. Her expression said she recognized him; they'd been introduced a couple of times. But something inside him told him that he recognized her, too. There was something about her. Something in those big brown eyes of hers that spoke to him. She wasn't just the quiet, reserved girl who worked at the doctor's office. She was someone who'd walked on the edge. She might not be there anymore, but she had a past—just like he did. He nodded, wondering if she felt it, too. Her curt nod suggested that maybe she did. She returned her attention to the treadmill and cranked it up until she was running at a fair pace.

Ivan's heart was racing far faster than his walking speed warranted. What he couldn't figure out was why. He'd seen her around, spoken to her a couple of times. He found her attractive. He'd known that since the first time he saw her. But from what he'd been told, and what she'd portrayed until tonight, she was quiet and reserved. A hometown girl who lived with her mom. Not the kind of girl he'd normally go for. But that look she'd just given him? Maybe he was imagining things? No. If he had to put money on it, he would. That had been the look of a woman who'd seen more of life than she should have. He rolled his shoulders and turned his head from side to side so he could take another peek. He needn't have worried. She was oblivious to him, gaze fixed ahead in a thousand-yard stare as she ran.

It wasn't the way a sweet, hometown girl ran to keep in shape. She looked more like a woman who was giving everything she had to keep just one step ahead of her demons.

~ ~ ~

Abbie checked her watch. Twenty-seven minutes done. She'd planned to run for an hour. Now she was in negotiations with herself. She should keep focused and run on, but it was hard to focus with that Ivan guy running a few yards to her left. She was surprised that she hadn't seen him in here before. His body made it obvious that he must spend a lot of time here. She did her best not to notice men these days. Most of the time, she succeeded, but there was something about Ivan. He was her type. Tall and dark and built. He wasn't conventionally handsome. He looked more like a street fighter than anything else, but there was something magnetic about him. She'd felt it the first time they were introduced. And because of that, she'd mostly avoided him since. Her days of hanging with the bad boys were over.

She looked at her watch again. Twenty-nine minutes. She could make up the time another day. Ivan was too distracting. She adjusted the controls and slowed the machine down to a walk. She'd cool off for a couple of minutes and then go and get changed and leave.

Of course, when she got off the treadmill, Ivan got down from his. He came toward her with a smile. Her breath caught in her chest. That was a very sexy smile. She couldn't help but smile back.

The silence lengthened while she looked into his eyes. She waited, not wanting to be the one to break it, wondering what he might say. There was no denying the electricity crackling in the air between them.

"Do you want to go get a drink?"

Even though she'd half expected it, his question sent a jolt of excitement through her. The way he looked at her made it clear that a drink wasn't all he wanted to have with her. Her stomach tightened at the thought of running her hands over his muscled chest, of his big arms closing around her and … She pulled herself together. "No."

He chuckled. "Wow. No hesitation whatsoever? Sorry. I read you wrong."

She couldn't help but smile back at him. "Don't apologize. And for what it's worth, I think you read me perfectly. That's why I said no so quickly. I'm not that girl anymore."

He nodded slowly. "I don't know who you were. I'd like to get to know who you are now."

She pursed her lips. There was something about him. He was like the guys she used to date. Sexy, upfront, but there was more to him than that. He felt like a kindred spirit—which was as crazy as it was undeniable. "The girl I am now wouldn't go out with a guy just like that, and she sure as hell wouldn't go home with him afterward."

He nodded again. "The guy I am now wouldn't ask you to go home with him afterward. But he would like to buy you a drink. Learn about why there's such a difference between who you were and who you are."

For some reason, she felt like he would understand. She shrugged. "Okay, then. Why not?" He was new in town. He'd only arrived a few months ago. Perhaps it'd do her good to make a new friend. "I'll meet you at the front desk in twenty minutes."

As she emerged from the locker room, she was negotiating with herself again. She shouldn't go with him, but if she did, she should stick with being the new Abbie—the new, improved version, the girl her mom was proud of. The girl who'd never let anyone down. The girl who didn't run around with bad boys.

Her stomach tightened again when she saw him waiting. He'd looked great in his workout gear. He looked just as good in dark jeans and a black leather jacket.

He smiled. "Do you want to go to the Boathouse?"

She thought about it. If people saw them there together, they'd be the talk of the town. She wasn't sure she wanted to face that.

He raised an eyebrow. "Someplace else?"

He had a point. That was the trouble with Summer Lake, there wasn't really anywhere else to go. Giuseppe's had a small bar, but the trouble with going there was that someone would see you anyway—and then the gossip would include the fact that you were sneaking around.

"You don't want to be seen out with me? You don't want people to talk?"

She gave him a rueful smile. "We're not going to give them anything to talk about, are we? The Boathouse is fine."

If she wasn't mistaken, he looked a little disappointed. She felt it, too. Part of her would like to suggest that they should go to his place—that way no one would see them, but they could do things that would make people talk if they knew.

~ ~ ~

As he watched Abbie slide into the booth and then took a seat opposite her, Ivan had to wonder what was going on here. She shrugged out of her jacket and gave him a questioning look. "What's up?"

He shrugged. "I'm not the kind to beat about the bush. I'm trying to figure you out."

"What do you want to know?"

"Like I said earlier—who you are, who you were, and why you talk as though that's two completely different people."

She held his gaze for a long moment. "Who do you think I am?"

"From what I've been told, from the little I've seen, you're Abbie. Sweet, hometown girl. A little quiet and reserved. You work at the doctor's office. You live with your mom. A good girl."

He didn't miss the smirk on her face before she covered it with her hand. "And that's who I am, these days."

The server greeted them with a smile. "Hi, guys. What can I get you?"

"I'll have a beer," said Abbie.

"Make that two," added Ivan.

"And can I get you some menus?"

"No, thanks." Abbie looked at Ivan. "Not for me, anyway."

"No. I'm good."

Once the girl had gone, he met Abbie's gaze again. "Who were you?"

She shrugged. "A girl who lost her way; let a lot of people down."

He nodded. "Mind if I ask what motivated the change?"

To his surprise, her eyes filled with tears.

He held up a hand. "Hey. I'm sorry. I don't mean to pry."

"Damn!" She swiped angrily at her face. "I'm sorry. I didn't think I'd react like that. This is going to sound crazy. I've been back here for just over a year. I've worked hard at becoming someone my mom can be proud of—someone I'm proud of, but ..." She shook her head. "Sorry. You seemed like someone who might understand. You probably think I'm nuts, some kind of psycho."

"Not what I was thinking at all. You seem like someone who's put herself under a lot of pressure to put up a front. I'm curious why."

She blew out a sigh. "I left town. Moved to the city. Had a lot of fun. Partied. You know. Went off the rails a bit. My parents were disappointed in me. Then ... then my dad died. I came back. I need to take care of my mom—be the daughter I should have been to both of them. I can't make it up to my dad. It's too late. But I can still make it up to my mom."

"I'm sorry."

The server came back and set their drinks down on the table. Abbie picked hers up and took three long gulps before she set it back down. "It is what it is."

"That's all anything ever can be."

"Yeah. Anyway, what about you? I know you work for Seymour Davenport, but you don't strike me as the kind of guy who took a direct route to becoming a chauffeur to a billionaire."

Ivan laughed. "No. I did anything but that."

She leaned her elbows on the table and leaned forward. Her dark hair fell around her face, and he had to resist the urge to tuck it back behind her ear. "What's your story?"

"I was in the army, military police. After I got out, I lost my way for a while. When I got clean, I was in a program that helps people get back on their feet, find work, a place to live. Mr. D hired me as his driver. I've done that for six years now. At least, until we moved up here. Now, he doesn't need me to drive for him, I'm helping run his charity office."

She nodded and took another drink. "I was right, then. You've walked on the dark side, too."

"Yeah. I guess we recognized it in each other."

She blew out a sigh. "So, I guess I haven't changed as much as I thought I had."

"I wouldn't say that. I believed that you were the quiet, reserved, live-at-home-with-momma girl until tonight." He wondered if he should tell her and decided that he would. "I thought you were hot, but not my kind of girl."

She raised an eyebrow at him. "Not your type?"

He let his gaze travel over her. She was tall and lean, long dark hair framed a pixie face. Exactly his type. "I don't mean physically."

She nodded. "You're not my type either. Not anymore."

The way she said it set his nerves on edge. The little hairs on the back of his neck stood up and sent a shiver down his spine. He smiled. "You don't mean physically either, do you?"

She gave him a sad smile. "I mean that the new Abbie wouldn't fool around with a guy like you."

He chuckled. "I'd love to know what the old Abbie would do."

She set her drink down. "I wish she were still around to show you. But you're the kind of guy …"

He shook his head. "I'm not, though, am I? I'm the new Ivan as much as you're the new Abbie. I'm not that guy anymore."

She gave him a sad smile. "Then I guess we can keep each other's secrets, huh?"

"I guess." For a crazy moment, he wanted to tell her that maybe he could help her figure out how to become a new version of herself without becoming someone else completely. It seemed to him that rather than bettering herself, she was denying who she really was. "Would you like to do more than that?"

"Like what?"

He smiled. "See each other again. Go out on a date."

She shook her head sadly. "We both know I'd be lying if I said I didn't want to, but I think it's best if we don't."

Ivan was surprised at the ball of disappointment that settled in his stomach. "Why?"

"Because we're too alike. You see who I am. And what you see is what I have to hide."

"Why hide it? You can't just become a whole new person; all you can do is become the best possible version of yourself. That's what I try to do, every day."

"Maybe you weren't all that bad, then. I was. I can't be that girl anymore." She looked into his eyes for a long moment and brought the bottle up to her lips and took a drink before she added, "And you make me want to be."

He shifted uncomfortably. She must have been deliberate in the way she'd taken a drink like that—either that or he was too horny after a long dry spell and was reading too much into it. She was teasing him at the same time she was saying she couldn't go there. He shrugged. He didn't want to play games. If her answer was no, he'd respect it. "So, is this new Abbie never going to date again?"

She made a face. "Someday, but only nice guys."

He chuckled. "Are you saying I'm not a nice guy?"

She gave him a rueful smile. "You're much nicer than I thought you'd be, and that makes you even more dangerous. I have to be responsible, sensible, and dependable, date a nice guy, get married and have two-point-four children. That's not what you're looking for in life. If we went out, it'd be for fun—and I don't doubt we could have a lot of fun, but I've already had my fair share; it's time for me to grow up."

Ivan nodded sadly. "Okay, you got me. I'm not asking you to marry me and produce offspring." He held his bottle up to her with a smile. "But if you want a friend in the meantime. If you want to talk to someone who understands how hard it can be to come in from the cold, I'll be around."

The way she smiled at him made him wonder for a second if he was admitting defeat too easily. But no. If she wanted to condemn herself to a life of domesticity and boredom, that was her choice. It wasn't a path he wanted to go down.

"I appreciate the offer. It's nice to think that there's someone in this town who I can be real with. You seriously wouldn't mind if I look you up sometimes when it all gets a bit much?"

"I wouldn't have offered if I minded." He smiled. "I'll buy you a drink and help you chase the blues away when trying to be someone you're not gets too much for you. But I still think you'd be better off just being who you are and making different choices. Better choices than you used to."

She held his gaze for a long moment. "You're probably right."

# Chapter Two

Abbie straightened the magazines on the coffee table and looked around the waiting room. It was all neat and straight and sanitized. It had been a busy week, and she was glad it was over. She didn't have to work tomorrow morning; she only did alternate Saturdays.

"Hey, Abbie." Michael smiled at her as he came out of his office. "Do you want to get out of here? It's almost time and if anyone comes in now, I can handle it."

"That's okay. I can wait."

"Nah, go on. Get off home. Do you have any plans for the weekend?"

She shrugged. "I want to get out for a run in the morning, but other than that, not much. How about you?"

He grinned. "We're dropping the boys off with my folks tomorrow and having a bit of a break."

"Aww, that's awesome. I know your mom loves having them, and you and Megan could use some time to yourselves. Are you going anywhere?"

"Yeah. We're going to have dinner at Giuseppe's tomorrow night and then go over to the Boathouse to meet up with everyone. I gave Meggie the choice of a romantic dinner by ourselves or catching up with the gang—so she chose both."

Abbie laughed. "Good for her! It's not often the two of you get out so you may as well fit in as much fun as you can."

"Absolutely. And what about you? You can go out as much as you like, but you don't seem to. Will you be at the Boathouse tomorrow?"

She shrugged. "Maybe. I'm not a hermit or anything. I go out for dinner with the girls on a Thursday sometimes."

"I know. But that's a bit more sedate. You should be out dancing and dating and … Oops. Sorry. I don't mean to tell you what you should be doing."

She smiled. "It's okay. I know you're not trying to tell me how to run my life."

"Hell, no!" He shook his head vigorously. "Wouldn't dream of it. I just don't like to think of you sitting home doing nothing. There's a great bunch of people around here. You should get to know them better, make friends. I know I was a couple of years ahead of you in school, but I remember you being really outgoing. You had tons of friends. I worry about what's going on with you that you're not like that anymore."

"I'm fine. Honestly. There's nothing wrong with me. I just prefer a quieter life these days."

"Yeah. I'm sorry, Abbs. You do your own thing."

"I might go tomorrow night. Roxy asked if I wanted to." She felt bad hearing that Michael worried about her. He and Megan had been so good to her since she'd come to work here at Michael's practice. She smiled. "I might see you there."

"Now, I feel like I nagged you into it."

She laughed. "You did no such thing. You're right. I deserve a night out. Mom's fine watching her shows on TV."

"Well, if I talked you into that, can I talk you into going home now? There are no more appointments and I'd like to get out early myself."

"Oh, in that case, of course." She went behind the reception desk and picked up her purse. "Consider me gone."

Michael shook his head. "You know, Abbs, you should really put as much effort into getting what you want as you do into helping other people get what they want."

She frowned, not understanding.

"When you thought I might need you, you were willing to stay as long as it took. Now you know I want to go home, you're out of here like a flash. I know it's not my place to say, but you're living your life around what you think your mom wants. What about you?"

She sucked in a deep breath and let it out slowly, making herself smile as she did. "Maybe what I want most is to see my mom happy and taken care of?"

Michael nodded. "I get that … but you can't tell me you don't want anything more than that—a life of your own?"

She laughed, hoping that it didn't sound too humorless. "I have a life of my own and I'm doing exactly what I want to with it. I did enough selfish stuff in the years I moved away from here."

Michael scowled. "Living your life isn't selfish."

She waved a hand at him. "You're not going to get out of here any earlier than usual at this rate. I'm fine. I appreciate your concern. Have a great weekend, and maybe I'll see you both tomorrow night."

"Okay, darl'." He smiled through pursed lips. "I get the message. I'll shut up and butt out."

Abbie felt bad as she walked back down Main Street. Michael was a good guy. He only wanted to see her happy. He just didn't get that she couldn't be happy if she wasn't putting her mom first. She had too much making up to do.

~ ~ ~

"Ivan!"

He looked around at the sound of a woman's voice calling his name and stopped when he spotted Chris standing beside her car across the street.

"Hey, Miss Chris." He hurried across the road, and she greeted him with a hug.

"Hey, yourself. How are you?"

"I'm doing great. How about you?"

She made a face. "Don't tell him I said this, but I'm missing Seymour."

Ivan laughed. "I won't tell if you don't; I miss him, too."

Chris laughed with him. "I didn't think about that. I've only been with him for a while, and this is the first time he's gone back to Montana. You've been with him for years, and it's the first time he's gone without you, isn't it?"

Ivan nodded. "Yeah. It's weird. I don't mind admitting that. I mean, it's good. I'm loving being in the office, and I'm glad that he trusts me enough to leave me in charge of everything here, but I can't help but worry about him driving himself around up there—especially at this time of year."

Chris shuddered. "I don't even want to think about it. So, I'm not going to. Where are you off to?"

"I just left work. I'm heading home."

Chris grinned. "What's for dinner?"

He raised his eyebrows. "I don't know yet."

She slipped her arm through his. "I don't either. So, rather than you going home and trying to figure something out, and me doing the same, do you want to have dinner with me?"

He grinned. "I'd love to."

When they got to the Boathouse, he held the door open for her, and they made their way to the bar.

Kenzie, the bartender, greeted them with a puzzled smile. "It's nice to see you both. Where's Seymour?"

"Montana," said Chris with a grin.

Kenzie laughed. "So, you two are keeping each other company in his absence?" She looked at Ivan. "You'll have to watch her, you know."

Ivan smiled. "I think I'm safe. Chris's only interest in me is that I'm someone she can talk to about Mr. D while he's not here."

Chris nodded happily. "It's true."

"Well, what can I get you?"

"Can we take a booth?" asked Chris. "We're here for dinner."

"Sure thing. Seat yourselves, and I'll bring your drinks and menus over."

Chris grinned at Ivan once they were seated. "I know why I'd be eating alone if it weren't for you. But what's your excuse? You've been here a couple of months by now. Why don't you have a hot date, or a pretty young thing waiting at home?"

Ivan made a face. "I do have a hot date."

Chris laughed. "Flattery won't get you anywhere with me. Come on. I'm serious. I thought you'd catch the Summer Lake bug when you moved here and find yourself a nice girl like everyone seems to."

He shrugged.

Chris narrowed her eyes at him. "What?" Her expression sobered. "I'm sorry. Am I being an idiot? I never thought. Would you be better off with a nice guy?"

Ivan chuckled.

Chris looked mortified. "I'm so sorry. I didn't even think."

"It's okay. I'm into girls, not guys. I'm just not looking for anyone right now."

Chris held his gaze for a moment. "Why not?"

He shrugged. "I don't know. I'm fine by myself. I'm getting to know this place. Learning my new job. There's been a lot of changes for me lately."

"So why not change it up even more and get yourself a nice girlfriend?"

He made a face. "I haven't met anyone I like that way."

"You haven't?"

He shook his head slowly. It wasn't exactly a lie. He'd met Abbie. He liked her. But he didn't like her that way, because there was no point. She wasn't interested in him. At least, not enough to do anything about it.

Chris gave him a sly smile. "The look on your face says you have, but you don't want to tell me about it."

"Nope. Only that there's nothing to tell."

"Okay." He was glad she let it go. He didn't mind her being nosey. That was just who Chris was, and he knew her intentions were good. He was glad she let it go because he didn't want to think about it too much. If he was honest—and he could do that with himself, if not with Chris—he wouldn't mind catching the Summer Lake bug, as she called it. Most of the guys he'd gotten to know here were coupled up, and he wouldn't mind his life going in that direction. Moving here was like starting a new chapter. He loved the way his new job was working out, loved that he wasn't always on the go like he'd been before. His days as Seymour's chauffeur had seen him splitting his time between Malibu, Montana, and the Caymans. It sounded cool—and it kind of was—but he was enjoying settling into small-town life.

Kenzie set their drinks down and handed Ivan a menu. "I know madam here is coming out with Clay and Marianne tomorrow night. Are you coming?"

Ivan met her gaze. He liked Kenzie. She struck him as someone who'd seen the darker side of life and lived to tell the tale, much like himself and, even though he wasn't supposed to be thinking about her, like Abbie. "Probably," he said, knowing that answer was less likely to get him into another conversation about how he should get a life.

"Good." Kenzie nodded. "Do you know what you want?"

He gave her a puzzled look. Was she reading his mind about Abbie?

"To eat," she added.

Once she'd gone, Chris smiled at him. "You might think you're safe now that I'm not going to bug you about finding a girlfriend, but I think Kenzie just adopted you."

He laughed. "Adopted me? She only asked if I'm coming out tomorrow night."

"You don't know Kenzie very well. You might as well accept your fate."

Ivan shook his head. "If she wants to play matchmaker, she can try."

"That's the spirit." Chris raised her glass to him. "She might just set you up with someone who's perfect for you."

Ivan lifted his glass with a smile. "She might." He doubted it, but all this talk about finding someone didn't sound so bad. After his drink with Abbie the other night, he had to admit that he did have some interest in dating. She might not be interested in him, but she had reminded him that he enjoyed going out with a woman. Maybe it was time he started.

~ ~ ~

"Good morning."

"Morning, Renée." Abbie tried to sound as bright and cheerful as she could. She'd come to the bakery to pick up her mom's favorite donuts, but she would have gone to the grocery store instead if she'd known that Renée was working this morning.

"How are things?"

She nodded. "Great, thanks. How about you?"

Renée ran the women's center. It was a great place, they offered all kinds of counseling—emotional as well as legal and financial. Abbie was grateful for all the help they'd given her since she came back to the lake. She'd had to deal with a lot—legally and financially to help her mom out. Her parents had never had much, but it turned out they did have quite a bit of debt. Renée had helped her take care of setting up payment plans and getting her mom's widow's pension. Abbie was grateful to her for all of it. It was hard to look her in the eye now, though. Renée seemed to know it, too.

"All's well here, thanks. What can I get you?"

Abbie forced a smile. It wasn't fair of her to be anything but sweetness and light with the woman who'd helped her save her parents' home. "Do you have any of the cinnamon donuts? Mom loves them."

"We do—or we will do in about eight minutes. There's a batch almost ready to come out of the oven. Do you want to have a coffee with me while we wait?"

Abbie was tempted to say no. To ask for something else and leave, but her mom did love those donuts.

"Sure. That'd be nice."

Renée poured them each a coffee and came around the counter. "Shall we sit?"

"Okay."

When they were seated, Renée blew out a sigh. "Mind if I ask you something?"

"Fire away." Abbie braced herself. She didn't know what was coming, but she doubted that she'd like it.

"Did I do something to piss you off?"

Crap! She'd thought she hid it so well. "No! Not at all. You've been so good to me. What makes you think that?"

Renée held her gaze for a long moment. "You avoid me as much as you can, and when you can't, you give me this fake nicey-nicey act. I don't get it. It's not you."

Abbie pursed her lips. "It's the new me. It's not fake. This is who I'm trying to be these days."

"Why?"

Abbie sighed. "Because I screwed up. I want to be better than I was."

"You already are. And it's not like you did anything horrible before anyway. I remember you in school. You were a few years behind me, but you were fun and outgoing and the life of the party. Now you're … different. You're nice to everyone, don't get me wrong, but it doesn't feel real."

Abbie shrugged. "Look what happened while I was off partying and having fun. I should have been here, and I wasn't.

Fun doesn't count for much in the grand scheme of things. I'm sorry. I guess I am edgy with you because you know just how bad things got for my folks while I was off having fun. I appreciate everything you've done for me, but honestly, I hate that you know the worst of it." There, she'd admitted it.

Renée gave her a sad smile. "You didn't cause any of it. It's just the way things worked out. Your folks were going through a tough time financially. Most people do at some point. It was just unfortunate that your dad passed before they could get through it. I was glad to be able to help you sort things out for your mom."

Abbie frowned. "They never should have been in such a mess. They wouldn't have been if I'd stayed here and done what I'm doing now. If I'd taken a job in town and lived at home, I could have contributed, and things would have been different."

"You can't blame yourself."

Abbie let out a short, bitter laugh. "I can, and I do."

"I wish you wouldn't. You couldn't have known what was going to happen, and I'm sure they wouldn't have wanted you to give up your own life."

"It is what it is. I can't change what happened, but I can try to make up for it now—to my mom, at least. I'm glad we've talked. I'll be honest, I avoid you as much as I can because I know what you must think of me."

"No!" Renée shook her head. "I get that you have to work through this in your time and in your own way, but I'm not going to let you set me up as the bad guy—for your sake, not mine. You can't keep telling yourself that Renée blames you or thinks you're a bad person. I'm not judging you. You're the one who's doing that. And you shouldn't. Avoid me if that makes life easier for you, but you won't get anywhere until you face up to the fact that you're the only one who thinks badly of you."

Abbie pressed her lips together. She wanted to argue. Wanted to tell Renée that she didn't need to take it easy on her. She was to blame, and she knew it.

But Renée was glaring at her. "You need to get your head straight, Abbie. Sometimes, life just sucks. Bad things happen. People die. And it's not anyone's fault. It's just the way life goes. There's no one to blame. Nothing that can be done to make amends. To use your own favorite phrase, it is what it is. And the sooner you understand that the sooner you'll be able to start living again. It's hard, it's sad. Believe me, I know, I understand. But you can't change the past, and you can't compensate for it. All you can do is live your best now and try to make a great future for yourself."

Abbie swiped angrily at the tears that pricked behind her eyes. "That's what I'm trying to do. I'm trying to be a better person."

Renée reached across the table and squeezed her arm. "You're trying to be a different person. You think that if you'd been someone else, your dad might not have died, and your mom wouldn't have been left in such a mess. But that's just not true. Just be yourself, Abbie. You'll never be happy otherwise. And no matter who you try to be, you can't change the past."

Abbie stared at her for a long moment. Part of her knew that Renée was right, but if she accepted that, she didn't know what she'd do with herself.

Renée checked her watch. "I'd better get those donuts out."

Abbie watched her get up and walk away. She turned before she disappeared in the back. "You came back to help your mom. What your mom needs more than anything is you—Abbie—the real one. Not some made-up character who you think she might like better than you."

Abbie had to swallow hard at that.

When Renée came back out, she set a bag of donuts down. "These are on me. I hope she enjoys them."

"Thanks."

"I'll say one more thing, then I'll butt out. If I can tell that you're putting on an act—and it hurts me because I thought we were closer than that—how do you think your mom feels?"

Abbie tried to blink away the tears. She couldn't speak, she just nodded, and picked up the donuts and left.

# Chapter Three

Ivan stepped out of the shower and toweled himself off. It was too early to get ready, but he had nothing else to do. He might as well make his way over to the Boathouse. He could hang out at the bar until people started to show up.

He rubbed the towel through his hair, then set it down on the countertop and leaned closer to the mirror. He should probably shave. He ran his hand over his cheek. Nope. It wasn't too bad, and it was damned cold outside. He met his gaze in the mirror and smirked. What was he, some kind of pussy? He didn't want to shave because his face might get cold on the ten-minute walk to the Boathouse? He shrugged.

The real reason that he didn't want to shave was a little deeper. It was one of the many minuscule forms of rebellion he allowed himself to indulge in. When he'd worked as Seymour Davenport's chauffeur, he'd had to be clean-shaven at all times. He'd been on standby pretty much twenty-four-seven. He hadn't minded that Mr. D could, and often did, call at any time of the day or night needing him to drive. What he had minded was that for a guy like him, it meant twice-daily shaving so that he always looked the part. Even before that, in his days in the military, shaving had been one of the many obligatory daily rituals. These days he had more freedom, and he liked to make the most of it. Of course, there had been what he now thought of as *the lost years*, the years when he'd lost his way and let himself go down a dark path.

He shook his head and ran a comb through his hair. Those days were long behind him, and he knew that he'd never go back to that dark place. But they were the reason that he only ever allowed himself mini rebellions.

The sound of his phone ringing downstairs brought his thoughts back to the present. Wrapping a towel around his waist, he hurried down to the kitchen to see who it was.

He smiled when he saw Colt's name on the display. "Evening, Deputy Stevens. What's up?"

"Hey, Ivan. Are you coming out tonight?"

"I am. Are you going to be there?"

"I sure am. I'm just kicking my heels killing time till I can go over there and not be way too early."

Ivan laughed. "I'm almost ready myself. Do you want to come over here first, and we can drink a beer before we go?"

"That'd be great."

"Awesome. Come whenever you're ready."

Colt laughed. "Is ten minutes too soon?"

"Nah. You're good. I'll be ready by then, but the front door's unlocked anyway … come straight in."

"Thanks. See you in a few."

Ivan hurried back upstairs to finish getting ready. He smiled at his reflection in the mirror and nodded. "Look at you. You're settling right into small-town life. Best buds with the deputy sheriff and everything."

When he was ready, he ran back downstairs and looked around the house. The last time Colt had been over here, he'd teased Ivan about living in this place. He'd had a point too. It was a great house, but much bigger than he needed and fancier than he needed, too.

He turned at the sound of a tap on the front door. "Come on in," he called.

Colt came in and grinned at him. "I see you still haven't done anything about making this place look lived in."

Ivan made a face. "What do you want me to do? All my stuff's here. I just don't have much. The furniture came with the place. It's not horrible—is it? I have no clue when it comes to that kind of thing."

"Horrible? It's awesome! You know I'm only kidding with you. It tickles me, that's all."

Ivan shrugged. "It makes me feel a little uncomfortable, if I'm honest. I mean, I'd feel more at home in one of the cabins at the resort. Mr. D set this place up for me. He said he wanted me to be able to make Summer Lake my home."

"I know. You're lucky. It must be nice to have a boss who sets you up with a fancy house on the water like this. I'd say he's done his part toward helping you make the lake your home. What makes me laugh is that you haven't done a damned thing to make this house your home."

"What am I supposed to? I moved in. My clothes are in the closet. I filled the fridge. I bought a TV."

"You've never lived any place for long before, have you?"

Ivan shrugged. "I guess not. I mean, in the years I've worked for Mr. D, I've lived in the guesthouse of his places. Before that, I was in the army." Ivan took a deep breath. Colt was a new friend, but he was becoming a good one. They'd each shared a little about their paths through life to this point. "In the years in between, I just kind of drifted, you know?"

Colt nodded, looking more serious. "Sorry. Yeah. To me, the way you live in this place is funny. I've lived in Summer Lake my whole life, apart from the academy. My house is full to overflowing with things I've collected over the years. Maybe after a few years here, you'll be the same."

"Maybe. I've never had much use for *things*."

Colt smiled. "And maybe you never will. Maybe I'm a packrat, and you're a neat freak. Or maybe, now that you're going to be in one place, you'll settle in and start collecting stuff."

"Nah. I'm not a collector."

Colt laughed. "Neither am I, but over time, stuff accumulates. At least, it does in my world. Anyway, you said you filled the fridge. Any cold beers waiting in there?"

"Yep. Come on through." Ivan led Colt to the kitchen, where he handed him a beer and popped the top off his own.

"Cheers." Colt raised his bottle.

"Cheers," replied Ivan. "I have to ask. Does the clutter at your place have anything to do with a woman?"

"Nope. There's no ex Mrs. Stevens who left me and left all her stuff behind. There's not even an ex-girlfriend who left her things at my place. Well, there are a few ex-girlfriends, but none I ever lived with. My clutter is all my own doing. I like to travel when I can, I bring back souvenirs." He frowned. "I dunno. I like art. I buy paintings. Up until now, I suppose I thought that everyone's the same—that we just accumulate stuff over the years. Now, instead of laughing at you, I'm starting to wonder if I'm just a slob."

Ivan laughed. "Somehow, I doubt that. We've just lived different lives, that's all. But now I'm settling into your world, and I don't mind telling you, I like this way of life. I wasn't sure if small-town living would suit me—but so far, I'm enjoying it."

"Good. I know it's not for everyone, but I love Summer Lake. I love my life here. I can't imagine living somewhere else. The only thing that's not so great is the dating scene."

Ivan raised an eyebrow. "You surprise me. I've heard about this so-called Summer Lake bug where everyone who comes here couples up and settles down happily."

Colt made a face. "That seems to be true for the people who move here—so you might be okay. It hasn't worked out that way for me, but it's different since I've lived here my whole life. I know everyone—I've always known them. The dating pool is pretty small." He chuckled. "And I wouldn't say this to many folks, but it could use some chlorine."

Ivan laughed. "Yeah, but is that only because, in your line of work, you don't get to deal with the nicest people in town?"

"Maybe. I don't know." He took a slug of his beer. "Maybe my luck will change soon."

"Is your biological clock ticking?" asked Ivan with a laugh.

Colt gave him a rueful smile. "Maybe it is. Or maybe it's just been too long since I got laid."

"Well, it's party night at the Boathouse. Who knows, maybe tonight's your night?"

"Probably not. But I'm not as much of a sad sack as I'm making myself out to be. I'm fine. I'm not desperate or anything."

Ivan grasped his shoulder. "Don't worry. I won't tell anyone."

Colt laughed. "It's hardly a secret. I think the whole town introduces me to any female visitor that comes to see them. They all have high hopes for me. Maybe I'm just too picky."

"Nothing wrong with being picky."

"What about you? Hasn't anyone caught your eye?"

Ivan shook his head slowly.

"And you're definitely not interested in Abbie?"

Ivan didn't want to lie. Colt knew from previous conversations that he thought she was hot.

"I know you think she's all prim and proper, but she didn't used to be."

Ivan let out a short laugh. "I ran into her earlier this week. We had a drink together after the gym. She told me a bit about herself—who she is now and who she used to be. I think she and I would have gotten along well before."

"Yeah, I can see that. But you're not interested in the new, more sedate version?"

"Doesn't matter if I am or not. She's not interested in me."

"Oh. Damn. Sorry."

Ivan laughed. "She didn't shoot me down or anything. She told me that I'm not the right kind of guy for the kind of life she has to live now."

Colt rolled his eyes. "I understood it when she came back. She wanted to be here for her mom, but it's been a long time now, and she's still trying to be this perfect, dutiful daughter."

"She told me."

"She did?"

"Yep."

"Wow! I'd guess she likes you more than she let on, then. Usually, all anyone gets out of her these days is a Stepford smile and inane conversation about nothing in particular."

"Yeah, well. All I really need to know is that she's not interested. Though she did say, she might look me up when she needs a friend."

"With benefits?"

Ivan's heart raced in his chest at the thought, but he already knew better. "Nah. Just as someone to talk to when putting on the goody-two-shoes act wears thin."

Colt held his gaze for a moment. "Depending on what you're interested in, that could be a much better option."

"Yeah." Ivan knew that much. If she'd wanted to sleep with him, he wouldn't have said no, but the fact that she saw him as a kindred spirit she could turn to … that meant a whole lot more.

~ ~ ~

Abbie sipped her water and smiled as she listened to the girls talk. Roxy had called her earlier and said that a few of them were going to have dinner together at the Boathouse and asked if she'd like to join them.

Her mom had been urging her to go out, and she knew that Michael would give her a hard time on Monday if she didn't go.

Maria turned to her with a smile. "How about you? You're quiet."

Abbie smiled, and Jade answered before she could say anything.

"Abbie's always quiet."

Abbie shrugged, and Roxy, who was sitting beside her, nudged her with her elbow. "You're not, are you?"

"Not always, no." She grinned at Jade. "I just don't talk as much as some people."

"Touché!" Jade grinned back at her. "Do you have a sister by any chance?"

"No. I'm an only child—is that what you're getting at?"

"No. I was thinking that usually when there are two sisters, one of them is quieter and one of them's more outgoing. Like Amber and me, or Megan and Kenzie."

"I can see the theory, but that's not my excuse. I guess I prefer to listen than to talk most of the time."

She didn't miss the puzzled look that Cassie gave her. She and Cassie had gone to school together. And now they worked together. Abbie tended to avoid her as much as possible; mostly because that was the tactic she'd adopted with everyone who had known her growing up, and also partly because Cassie was such an obvious success, while she herself wasn't.

She was grateful that the conversation moved on when Roxy spotted some of the guys coming in. "Uh-oh. Looks like the girls-only part of the evening might be coming to an end here shortly."

Angel smiled and waved at her fiancé Luke who had come in with Zack and Logan.

Maria looked around the table. "I don't think any of us mind too much, do we?"

Jade laughed. "I think that will depend on who you ask. Those of you whose guys just walked in won't mind at all. The rest of us will either wish it was just a girls' night or be anxious to see which eligible single guys are out tonight."

"True," answered Maria. "And which camp do you fall into?"

Jade smiled. "The second one. You know that. I enjoy getting together with you ladies, but I always like to see which guys are out. Mostly just as eye candy, but you never know, one day, a tall dark handsome stranger might walk in and sweep me off my feet."

Amber laughed. "That'll be the day. If any guy ever tried to sweep you off your feet, you'd probably punch him in the mouth for being so chauvinistic."

Jade laughed with her. "Probably. But you know what I mean."

"Isn't there anyone local who's caught your eye?" asked Cassie.

"Sure. I think Ivan's gorgeous. I mean, look at him." Jade jerked her head toward the bar where Ivan and Colt had joined the other guys.

Abbie's heart raced. He was gorgeous. He was tall and dark, and tonight he had the kind of scruff on his face that wasn't quite a beard. It made him even more attractive in her eyes. It made him look rougher—more her type than when he was clean-shaven and dressed in a suit. Worse than that, it set her imagination running wild. She could feel the roughness of that scruff against her skin. She pulled herself together.

"He's single, isn't he?" asked Cassie. "Why don't you ask him out?"

Jade laughed. "Nah. He's not my type. Looking is one thing, but … I dunno. He's a nice enough guy, but he doesn't do it for me."

Abbie shuddered. Ivan sure as hell did it for her.

Roxy nudged her again. "I thought you liked him?"

She shook her head rapidly. She couldn't admit it, but she couldn't make herself deny it. She shot a glance in his direction and noticed that another guy had joined him and Colt. "Who's that?"

Roxy and the others all looked.

"That's Neil," said Cassie. "He's a sweetheart. He's an accountant."

"He looks nice." Abbie watched him as he chatted with the other guys. He did seem nice—in a sensible, dependable kid of way.

"I could introduce you if you like? He's single."

Abbie turned to look back at Cassie. "Maybe later?" Her heart was racing again, though unfortunately it wasn't at the thought of meeting Neil. It was more the thought of Cassie introducing them right under Ivan's nose. She'd told him she wasn't interested in him—and she wasn't, he didn't fit in with her life plan. Neil? He just might.

"Of course," Cassie said with a smile.

It didn't take long before half the table had emptied. It was only to be expected that the girls were eager to see their men. No doubt later, the table would fill up again as they came to sit down. For now, Abbie found herself sitting with Cassie and Amber.

"So, did you grow up here as well?" Amber asked Cassie.

"I did."

"But you two don't know each other?"

Cassie looked at Abbie. "I was a couple of years ahead of Abbie in school."

"Yeah, and we lived on opposite sides of town," added Abbie. Cassandra Stevens had grown up in one of the big houses up on the north shore, while she had lived in the same little two-bedroom rancher in town where she still lived now.

"Okay." Amber looked puzzled. "And now you work together?"

"Not really," Abbie answered before she stopped to think about it. "Cassie's the doctor, I'm just the receptionist."

Cassie gave her a puzzled look. "Wow! I'd have said yes, we do work together, and I couldn't do my job without you."

Abbie pursed her lips. "Sorry. That wasn't meant to be a dig at you." She blew out a sigh. "I'm sorry. I'm not a bitch, really. I guess I'm a bit down on myself. You went off to train to become a doctor, and now you're back here doing your part for the town. I went off and didn't make anything of myself, and now I'm back trying to make up for the mess I left behind." She bit her lip. She shouldn't have said that much. Shouldn't have been so honest.

Cassie reached out and touched her arm. "I'm sorry about your dad. That must be so hard."

Abbie had to swallow a couple of times before she spoke. "It is. But it's no excuse for me to act like that. I'm sorry. I think you're amazing. You've done so well for yourself, and I suppose I'm a bit jealous."

"There's no need to apologize. And for what it's worth, although I won't deny that I'm proud of myself for my career, it well and truly screwed up my personal life. The grass is always greener, but we're all struggling in our own ways."

Abbie nodded. She hadn't known Cassie well in high school, but she'd always seemed like a kind person, a good person. "Yeah. I think sometimes I forget that I'm not the only one who's struggling. I think I walk around under a dark cloud sometimes."

"How about I introduce you to Neil?" Cassie smiled. "Maybe dating a nice guy would help you chase the blues away?"

Abbie glanced over at the bar. Neil was still there, talking to Austin, but Ivan was nowhere in sight. "Thanks, I'd like that."

As they made their way over to the bar, Cassie linked her arm through Abbie's. "You know, I thought you had something against me since you came to work at the practice."

Abbie squeezed her arm. "I'm sorry. I don't have anything against you. I think I have something against myself for screwing up my life so badly."

"You haven't screwed anything up."

Abbie wasn't about to start arguing. She knew the truth, and she didn't need to convince Cassie or anyone else.

"Hi, Neil. It's nice to see you out."

"Hi, Cassie, it's good to see you, too." He smiled at Abbie. He had fair hair and blue eyes, not a look that had ever done it for her. But he did have a kind smile.

"I'm sorry," said Cassie. "This is Abbie. Abbie, this is Neil Donavan."

He held out his hand, and Abbie shook with him.

"Nice to meet you."

"The pleasure's all mine." He smiled a little too eagerly.

"Fresh drinks, ladies?" Kenzie grinned at them from behind the bar. "What can I get you?"

"Whatever they want, it's on me," said Neil.

"Actually," said Cassie. "I still have mine. I'll go get it." She winked at Abbie and left her standing there with Neil.

# Chapter Four

Ivan pulled his hat farther down over his ears. Coming out for a run this morning was probably a bad idea. It was too damned cold! But it was still a better idea than sitting in the house staring out at the lake and stewing about Abbie and Neil.

He'd choked on his drink last night when he'd seen the two of them standing at the bar talking. Neil was a nice enough guy. He was personable, friendly. Ivan set his jaw and started jogging down the driveway. Hell, Ivan himself had told him just the other week at work that he was a great guy who one day would find himself a great girl.

He hadn't suspected at the time that Neil might find the very girl who Ivan was interested in. And by the way it had looked last night, Neil was having much more success with her. There'd been no sign of the defeated, cynical chick Ivan had had a drink with last week. Around Neil, she'd been animated and flirty, flicking her long dark hair back over her shoulders and laughing at whatever Neil said.

He sprinted the last hundred yards to the gate, then huffed and panted to himself while he tapped in the code to unlock it and let himself out. Even in his current agitated state, he was still amazed and thankful that he lived in such a great place. He wasn't a newbie when it came to electronic gates and security systems and beautiful houses in the best part of town. But this was the first time that it was his own house. He'd lived like that previously in the guest house of Mr. D's place. Now his very own home was something he would never have dreamed about not so long ago.

He forced himself to smile as he locked the gate and started jogging toward the end of Main Street. He was lucky that he got to live this life. He wasn't going to spoil his Sunday morning run just because a girl he was interested in preferred his colleague, the accountant.

He smiled as he saw a figure appear a little farther along the street. He lengthened his stride and ran faster to catch up.

"Morning, Dan."

Dan turned and nodded. "Hey, Ivan. I haven't seen you in a while."

Ivan chuckled. "I'm not a fan of the cold. I've been hitting the gym more instead of running."

"And yet you chose one of the frostiest mornings to come out?"

Ivan shrugged. Dan was like that. He noticed little details. He wasn't calling you out on your bullshit, but sometimes it felt that way. "I need to clear my head. Fresh air helps with that in a way that the gym never seems able to."

"I can see that. I'm on my five-mile route this morning. Want to join me?"

Ivan nodded. He'd only planned to run three, but he'd skipped too much lately, and besides, Dan was good company. "Sure, if you don't mind?"

Dan smiled. "Do you have much to talk about?"

"I might blow off steam about a chick if you can stand it?"

Dan held up a pair of earbuds. "I have these if it gets too much."

Ivan laughed. Dan was one of those guys who didn't say too much, but when he spoke, it was worth paying attention. He was one of the smartest people Ivan had ever met. "You can just tell me if I get too annoying."

Dan stretched his quads and nodded. "Okay." He set off at a jog toward the park at the end of the street.

Ivan jogged after him. Maybe he didn't need to talk at all. Maybe he should just follow Dan's example and run in silence, focus on moving his body instead of agitating his mind.

He was still working on that when they reached the other side of the park.

"Want to take the old road?" asked Dan.

"Yep."

Once they reached the top of the rise, Dan glanced over at him. "Did you change your mind?"

Ivan raised an eyebrow.

"About bending my ear?"

"No, I just figured you were only being polite."

"No. My version of polite would have been to tell you that I needed to run by myself. I find it easier to speak the truth—and it's much more polite."

"Sometimes, I forget that you're more straightforward than most people."

Dan smiled. "I think the preferred term for people like me is socially awkward."

Ivan laughed. "I'd say it's more like socially advanced—you're so far above the usual bullshit that you don't lower yourself to take part in it."

Dan's lips quirked up in the hint of a smile. "I like to help when I can. You sounded as though you needed to let off some steam. Often all that's needed is someone to listen. I don't mind doing that."

"Thanks." Ivan felt dumb. It wasn't as though there was anything going on between him and Abbie. She'd made it clear that there wouldn't ever be.

"Can I ask who she is?" Dan didn't even turn to look at him as they ran down the other side of the rise.

"Abbie."

"I see."

"Do you? Do you know her?"

"She works at Michael's office? Grew up here?"

"Yeah. That's her."

"And what's the problem?"

"There really isn't one. I'm being an idiot. She doesn't like me. Well, she admitted that she does, but told me that she wouldn't ever go out with me."

Dan frowned. "That doesn't make sense."

"It does when you know a bit more. She ..." He thought about it for a few moments. It wasn't his place to share her story with anyone, not even Dan, who he knew wouldn't breathe a word of it. "She's only into nice guys now."

"You're a nice guy."

"Thanks. I think so, too. But I don't mean like that. I mean more ... I don't know. To use her own words, sensible, dependable. She wants someone she can marry and have two-point-four children with and live a respectable little life."

"And you don't want that?"

"That's not who I am."

Dan shot him a puzzled look. "So, you're incompatible. It's sad, but it happens. You wouldn't be happy if you had to compromise who you are to be who she wants. And vice versa."

"I know, but it's not that straightforward."

"It isn't?"

"No. Because that's not who she really is, and it's not what she really wants. It's who she thinks she should be. She wants to be a good girl and live a good life, but she's not like that."

Dan ran on in silence for a while. For so long that Ivan started to wonder if he wasn't going to comment. Eventually, he turned and met Ivan's eye. "The way I see it, if she's trying to be someone she isn't, and trying to live a life that doesn't really suit her, it'll all fall apart at some point. You have two choices. You can try to convince her that she's wrong—and a word of advice—a woman will never thank you for doing that. Or you can wait until she figures it out for herself and help her pick up the pieces when she does."

Ivan mulled it over. Dan was right, of course. He already knew that himself. He couldn't convince her that the way she was going about her life was all wrong. He'd already offered to be her friend when the going got tough. What he hadn't expected was that it would bother him so much when she met a guy who fit the picture of what she said she wanted. Of course, it didn't help that Ivan worked with that guy every day.

"I know you're right."

"So, why are you having a hard time accepting it?"

"Because last night she met a guy who fits the bill. A guy who is sensible and dependable, and I'm sure he would be very happy to settle down with her and live a nice little life with two-point-four children."

"Ah."

"Yeah."

"But if that isn't who she is, it will all fall apart."

"I know. But I don't want to see her—or him—get hurt in the process. And besides, I'm jumping the gun. I don't know what will happen between them."

"But it's eating you up inside that something might?"

Ivan blew out a sigh. "Yeah. It is."

"In that case, I see a third option for you."

"You do? What is it?" Ivan knew he sounded too eager, but he couldn't help it.

"You need to show her that you're what she really wants and that life with you would suit her better than whatever she might build with this other guy."

"But …"

"I know. That wouldn't be an easy thing to accomplish, but it's an option."

They ran on in silence. Dan seemed to have spoken his piece, and Ivan had a lot of thinking to do.

When they finally entered the park again on their way back, Dan slowed to a walk and checked his watch before looking at Ivan. "Are you any clearer?"

Ivan shrugged. "I'm clearer about my options—thanks to you. But I'm no clearer on which I should choose."

"Well, you know where I am if I can be of help."

"Thanks, you've done enough. I'll figure it out."

"I'm sure you will. Miss and I are going to the Boathouse for breakfast in a little while. Do you want to come?"

"Thanks, but I need to shower, and I have some work to do."

"Okay. I'll see you around." Dan lifted a hand and jogged toward the other side of the park, headed home.

Ivan walked the rest of the way back. He was toying with the option of stepping up and showing Abbie who he was in the hopes that she would recognize he was a better match for her than Neil. It might save her from herself and her idea that she had to be someone she wasn't. On the other hand, it would mean going against Neil—competing with him—and he didn't like that idea one bit.

By the time he got home, he'd almost convinced himself that he should just forget about her. That might be better for everyone—including himself. After all, there was no guarantee that she'd want him even if he did put himself out there and make a play for her.

~ ~ ~

"What do you think, should I make us a roast this afternoon?"

"I told you, I can pick us something up from the resort. That'd be cheaper than doing a roast, and it'll mean that you don't have to stand in the kitchen cooking for hours."

"I don't mind. I enjoy it." Abbie's mom smiled at her and pushed the cart toward the produce aisle. "I can do mashed potatoes and roast and make some of that gravy you like."

Abbie sighed. There was no point in arguing. Just because she thought her mom would be better off putting her feet up and watching a movie on a Sunday afternoon, it didn't matter. Her mom loved to make a full roast dinner. It reminded Abbie too much of her dad. In the old days, when she was still in high school, she and her dad would watch the game on TV while her mom cooked. Now, she felt as though she should be the one cooking, taking care of her mom instead of lounging around watching TV. But she wasn't much of a cook, and her mom wouldn't hear of it anyway.

They carried on, making their way up and down every aisle. Her mom liked to do it that way because she spotted all the deals on the end caps that she might miss otherwise. It drove Abbie nuts—she wished that they didn't need to search for deals, and she wanted to get out of here as soon as possible. Grocery shopping was not her idea of fun, but it was her mom's. So, she tried to make her smile as genuine as possible when her mom held up a can of tomato soup.

"Look. They're two for one. We can have them with grilled cheese in the week."

"Great." Abbie wished she could afford to get them takeout from the Boathouse for dinner. But that wasn't in the budget. To be fair, their budget was a lot less limited now than it had been when she first came home. Her mom had been drowning in debt. But Abbie had worked her butt off to set up payment plans and to make the money to meet them. Things were better now that she was working for Michael. Her salary was a lot more than she'd been making in the two jobs she'd worked before. One day, in the not too distant future, some of the smaller debts would be paid off, then she'd be able to make bigger payments to the other ones and still have a little more left over.

"Abbie?" Her mom's voice pulled her out of her thoughts.

"What?"

"Did you even hear me? Do you know him?"

"Who?" She looked up to see Ivan standing at the end of the aisle, smiling at her. "Oh. Yeah." She raised a hand and gave him a brief nod before turning to her mom. "He's just a guy from the gym."

Her mom waggled her eyebrows. "I wouldn't mind seeing him work out!"

"Mom!"

"What? He's sexy. You can't tell me you don't think so."

Abbie shrugged. "He's okay. I suppose."

"I know you better than that, young lady. You like him, don't you? Is he the one who walked you home last night? Don't think I didn't hear you."

Shit! She'd hoped that her mom was fast asleep when Neil had walked her to the front door last night. He hadn't kissed her or anything. She still wasn't sure why.

"Here he comes. Don't worry. I won't tell him that I heard you."

"It wasn't him!"

"Oh!" Her mom made a face that Abbie knew meant she was disappointed. "That's a shame."

"Hey, Abbie."

"Hi, Ivan." She hoped that he might keep on walking. No such luck.

He turned to her mom and held out his hand. "You must be Abbie's mom. It's nice to meet you. I'm Ivan."

Her mom, God bless her, batted her eyelashes at him as she shook his hand. "It's lovely to meet you. I'm her mom. You call me Nina."

Abbie rolled her eyes. She wanted this to be over. She didn't want her mom taking a liking to him. That wouldn't do at all. Abbie already liked him more than she should, but he wasn't the kind of guy she needed in her life. She needed someone more … she didn't even know what the right words were. Sensible and dependable were the words she'd said to him, but she had no proof that he wasn't either of those. He was too sexy; he'd taken a walk on the dark side. He wasn't … she sucked in a deep breath. He wasn't an accountant who was looking to settle down. That was what she needed, and she'd met one of those just last night. All right, so he might not melt her insides the way Ivan was doing right now, but he was more … more … suitable.

"Did you have a good time last night?"

Abbie's head snapped around to meet his gaze. She hadn't expected him to ask about that.

"I did, thanks. Did you?"

His blue eyes seemed to darken as he nodded. "It was all right."

Abbie was acutely aware of her mom watching them. The silence lengthened. She wished he'd just continue on his way, but he was still looking into her eyes, and for some reason, she couldn't drag hers away.

"Are you going out tonight?" Her mom's question broke the spell, and Abbie turned to look at her.

"No. You know that."

"You should." She smiled at Ivan. "You two should go out for a drink. You'd be doing me a favor. I have a whole pile of sewing I want to get to, but I take up the whole living room when I get my machine out, and Abbie doesn't like it."

"I don't mind!"

Her mom smiled at her. "You should go out."

To Abbie's surprise, Ivan nodded. "I'm game, if you are. I can come and pick you up around seven."

Abbie stared at him then looked back at her mom, who was nodding happily. "That'll be perfect. It'll give me a few hours to get some work done."

"Okay." Ivan raised an eyebrow at Abbie. "I'll see you at seven?"

She nodded. She didn't know how to say no without turning it into a big deal. "Okay."

"Well, we'd better get done with our shopping. It was lovely to meet you, Ivan. I'm sure I'll see you soon." With that, her mom pushed the cart away down the aisle.

Abbie scowled at Ivan, but he just smiled. "I'll see you later," he said before turning on his heel and going back the way he came.

"Mom!" Abbie scolded when she caught up with her. "What do you think you're playing at?"

Her mom smiled happily. "Getting myself some good sewing time—and getting you a night out with Ivan. It's obvious he likes you, and it's obvious you like him. What's the problem?"

"The problem ... the problem is ..." How could she explain it? The problem was that Ivan was far too attractive for her own good. He was the kind of guy who she'd wanted to party with, to stay up talking till dawn with. The kind of guy she'd like to take off with for the weekend and see where the road led them. He was not the kind of guy who would want to set up home with her and stay here at the lake. He wasn't the kind of guy who her mom would be happy to see her with—or at least she hadn't thought so.

"Is what?" asked her mom, innocently.

Abbie blew out a sigh. "The guy who walked me home last night is an accountant. He just moved here not long ago. He's looking to settle down and make a life here."

"And?"

"And that's the kind of guy I need."

Her mom scowled. "The kind of guy you need is one who looks at you the way Ivan does. No matter who you choose, you'll settle down together at some point. If you start with fireworks, you'll settle down to glowing embers that will keep your hearts warm forever. But if you start with only mild enthusiasm, you'll end up with cold ashes that will darken your heart."

Abbie stared at her for a long moment. She had no idea that her mom saw things that way. She had so many questions, but she only asked the most important one. "Did you and Dad start with fireworks?"

Her smile said it all. Her eyes glistened as she nodded. "We did. And we kept those embers pretty hot, too. I know that's too much information about your parents, but it's important, Abbie. I've been worried about you lately. You've turned into this dutiful dowdy daughter, and I know it's my fault. I appreciate everything you've done for me, but I won't let you give up your whole life just to make mine better. I know I fell apart for a while after your dad, but I have to find my own way in life now. You do, too. You have to find your path—and it should be one that makes you happy."

Abbie didn't know what to say. "I am happy. I'm happy being back here with you, and I'll be happy to stay here with you, maybe get married and live just down the road and have babies so that you'll have grandkids to play with."

Her mom shook her head firmly. "You'd only ever be happy with that if it's what happens for you and the man who makes you happy. You can't try to find someone who you think fits that mold. It won't work."

Abbie shrugged. She didn't want to be having this conversation at all, let alone in the middle of the grocery store. "Well, I'm not going to figure out what to do with myself standing here. Shall we finish shopping?"

Her mom looked as though she wanted to say more, but she just nodded.

When they were almost done, her mom swiped a box of Christmas decorations from the end cap near the checkout. "Do you think we should get a tree?"

Abbie closed her eyes. She'd always loved decorating the tree. But it was something they'd done as a family—the three of them. She shook her head slowly. "I know you hate the artificial ones."

"Oh, I do. I didn't mean one of those. I meant, should we get a real one? I heard that Jim is going to be setting up his lot in the square next weekend."

"We could. I suppose. A small one, maybe."

"No! We need at least a six-footer."

"We can't mom. I have no idea how I'd get it home and set up."

"We could manage it between us."

"I don't think so. But we don't have to decide right now. Let's get out of here and go home. I'll give Jim a call in the week and see if he can do anything about getting it delivered."

"Okay. You're right. We should get going. I need to get this roast made so that you can eat before your date tonight."

"It's not a date."

Her mom just smiled.

# Chapter Five

Ivan brought the car to a stop in front of Abbie's house at five minutes before seven. He'd spent years of his life making sure that Seymour arrived ten minutes early to all his appointments. The habit was deeply ingrained. He'd tried hard to make sure that he arrived here on time, but five minutes early was better than ten.

He cut the ignition and rubbed his sweaty palms together. He was nervous. This was a crazy move. He'd had to push himself to go and talk to them in the grocery store this morning. If Abbie's mom hadn't been so encouraging, he would likely have chickened out. But here he was. He knew Abbie would probably be mad at him—and not afraid to tell him so, once her mom wasn't around, but still. This was the opportunity he needed. Now to see whether he could make something of it, or whether he'd blow it.

He got out and walked up the path to the front door. He raised his hand to knock, but the door opened before he could.

"Ivan! Come on in. She's almost ready." Abbie's mom greeted him with a smile.

"Thanks."

He stepped into the hallway, and she smiled up at him. "Are you all ready for Christmas?"

That caught him by surprise. He hadn't given any thought to what he'd do for Christmas. "Not yet," he answered. "Are you?"

She smiled. "Not quite, no. We are going to have a tree this year, though."

Ivan smiled back, not sure what to say to that.

Luckily, Abbie appeared at the top of the stairs. "Oh! You're here already. I didn't hear the door."

"That's okay," said her mom. "I was just telling Ivan about the tree. Maybe he can help us get it here from the lot."

Abbie scowled at her. "The lot doesn't even open till next weekend, Mom."

Ivan had to hide a smile at the wink her mom gave him when she looked up at him. "So, maybe next weekend, you can help us with the tree?"

"Of course. I'd be happy to help." From what Abbie had told him about her mom and about her situation, he'd expected someone quite formal and intimidating—a woman who had high standards for her daughter. Instead, she was a sweet lady who seemed to very much approve of him.

Abbie frowned at him but didn't say anything.

"Great. Thank you so much," said her mom. "Anyway. You two get going, don't let me hold you up."

Ivan looked at Abbie, and she nodded. "Yeah. Let's go."

When they reached his car, Ivan held the door open for her, and she raised an eyebrow at him. "You're driving?"

"It's so cold. I didn't want you to freeze on the way home."

"Thanks." She got in, and he closed the door. "Where are we going?" she asked when he got into the driver's seat.

"I figured we'd just go to the Boathouse. You said just a drink. But we can eat if you haven't."

She made a face. "My mom said a drink, not me. And I have eaten."

He pursed his lips. She sounded pissed, and to be fair, he could understand why. As much as he wanted a shot to show her who he was—and as much as he hoped she'd realize that he was the kind of guy she wanted to go out with, he didn't want to force her into it.

He turned to look at her. "I know your mom kind of set you up with this. We don't have to go anywhere if you don't want to."

She narrowed her eyes at him. "We do. We have to go somewhere because I am not spending the evening sitting there listening to that damned sewing machine and her country music. She's all set to enjoy herself—and that's not my idea of fun."

He chuckled. "Okay. The Boathouse, then?"

She made a face.

"No?"

"I don't know if you noticed, but last night, I was in there talking to another guy."

Ivan's smile disappeared. "I noticed."

She didn't pick up on the change in his tone. "Yeah, well, if you did, don't you think everyone else did?"

"I guess."

"So, I don't want to be that chick who's seen in there with a different guy every night."

He almost asked why it would be a problem—if she only saw him as a friend. But he managed to keep his mouth shut. Instead, he waited.

"So, I guess that means your place. The Boathouse is a no go, and Giuseppe's would be even worse."

His heart raced. When they'd talked about where to go for a drink last week, he'd almost suggested that they should go to his place. He hadn't, but only because he had the feeling that once they were behind closed doors, things might move a little too fast.

She raised an eyebrow at him. "Or not?"

He slid the key in and turned the ignition. "My place it is."

"Are you freaking kidding me?" she asked when he stopped in front of the gate and pressed the remote. She watched wide-eyed as it swung back, and he pulled forward.

"About what?" For the first time, it occurred to him that the house might impress her. Instead of being happy that he had that on his side, it made him frown. Now, if she was more open to him, he'd wonder if it was because she liked him or because she saw him as a more viable option. She wanted to settle down and build a respectable little life. Would she see this place as more respectable—more desirable? And if she did, would he still respect her?

He pulled the car into the garage and looked over at her. "The house comes with the job. It's not mine."

She gave him a puzzled look. "What do you—oh! Asshole!"

"Excuse me?"

"You think I'm going to change my mind about you—set my sights on you because you live in a big fancy house?"

"No!"

She shook her head and blew out a sigh. "What are we even doing? You don't seem to think very much of me. Maybe I should just walk over to the Boathouse, by myself."

"No! Abbie. I'm sorry. I don't know what I'm doing here, other than screwing this up, but please, stay? Have a drink with me? Hang out?"

Her expression softened.

"Please?"

She nodded and smiled. "You're as hopeless as I am when it comes to this stuff, aren't you?"

A wave of relief washed through him. "Yeah. Probably worse."

~ ~ ~

Abbie pulled up a seat at the island in the kitchen while Ivan went to the fridge. He came back and popped the top off a beer before setting it down in front of her.

"Thanks." She took a big gulp and looked up at him, wondering what he was thinking.

He gave her a rueful smile. "If you're going to ask me what I'm doing—what I'm playing at—I can't tell you, because I don't know."

She watched him take a drink. His long fingers curled around the bottle, the muscles under his shirt flexing as he lifted his arm. Her stomach tightened. Damn. He had that effect on her every time she looked at him. She wished he didn't. It was hard not to compare him to Neil. Neil didn't have the same effect. He …

"What are you thinking?"

She pursed her lips. She could hardly tell him. "I don't know what to think. I told you last week that this, you and me? It's not a good idea."

"I know, but I don't understand why. I thought I kind of understood. I thought that I was someone your mom wouldn't approve of—but now we both know that's not true."

Abbie couldn't help but smile. "Yeah. She's taken quite a shine to you."

"But you haven't?"

She froze as he reached out and tucked a stray strand of hair behind her ear. His fingertips grazed her neck and sent waves of excitement rushing through her. "Don't!"

He pulled his hand back as if he'd been scalded. "Sorry."

"So am I! I'm not going to deny that I find you attractive."

The corners of his lips turned up, and his gaze locked with hers. His blue eyes were dark, like a stormy ocean—and that's what she felt she'd be drowning in if she allowed herself to get close to him. He was sexy-as-sin. She had no doubt that he'd be a whole lot of fun—both in bed and out of it. But he wasn't the kind of guy who was looking to settle down. She didn't need another boyfriend, didn't need to waste any more of her life with a guy who was only looking for the good times. She needed someone who was ready for the kind of life that she needed at this point.

"In case you didn't know, I find you attractive, too, Abbie. Very attractive." He dropped his gaze, and the way his eyes lingered on her lips felt as though he was commanding them to kiss him.

She wanted to. She could feel herself start to lean toward him, but with a massive effort of will, she managed to stop. "I did know." She got down from the stool and paced away from him, needing to put some distance between them and break the spell it felt like he was casting over her. "I knew it was there, between us, the first time we met. Then, last week in the gym, it was obvious." She shook her head. "It was obvious to me that I should stay the hell away from you."

"Why?" He'd followed her and now stood facing her. Her back was to the cabinets, and he stood between her and the doorway.

She closed her eyes. "Because …" She took a step toward him and looked up into his eyes. "Because you bring out the worst in me."

He stepped forward, closing the gap between them and resting his hands on the counter on either side of her hips. He was caging her in, but she didn't want to escape. She put her hands on his chest, and he closed his arms around her waist and drew her against him. Her heart hammered in her chest as she slid her arms up around his neck and he held her closer, pressing his hard body against hers and making her forget why she wasn't supposed to be doing this.

"Maybe I could bring out the best in you?" He raised an eyebrow.

She had a feeling that he might. The way her body was humming with desire for him told her that good things were about to happen. Her head was fighting a losing battle, and the little voice of reason gave up as he cupped her cheek in one hand and lowered his lips to hers.

At first, he was tentative, as if he still wanted to give her the option to stop. She should, some little part of her knew that. But her fingers didn't want to listen as they sank into his hair and pulled his head down. The moment his tongue slid into her mouth, the battle was lost. She kissed him back hungrily, her hands roving over his back and shoulders. She moaned when his hands closed around her ass and pulled her closer against him. His hard-on pressed into her belly, igniting a desire inside her that she already knew could only be satisfied one way. She rocked her hips against his letting him know that she wanted the same thing he did.

He kissed her more deeply but didn't make any attempt to take things further. She rocked her hips more urgently, hoping he'd take the hint, but when he didn't, she made the move herself, reaching for his zipper.

He lifted his head and looked down into her eyes. He looked cautious, but not so much that he stopped her from sliding her hand inside his shorts and closing her fingers around him. He was rock hard, thick, and hot. She moved her hand up and down his length, loving the way his eyes glazed with lust.

"This wasn't what I planned," he breathed.

She chuckled. "I know, it's what we were both trying to avoid. But here we are."

He opened his eyes and pulled her skirt up around her waist. "Here we are," he echoed. "Are you sure this is what you want?"

She tightened her fingers around him. "Absolutely sure. So, do you want to keep talking about it or—" She didn't get a chance to finish the question as he lifted her up and sat her on the edge of the counter.

She wriggled out of her panties and watched as he pushed his jeans and boxers down.

He held her gaze as he trailed his fingers over her entrance, then slid them inside her. She was soaking wet for him, and it felt so good that she moaned. But it wasn't his fingers she wanted.

She held her arms open to him, and he stepped between her legs. She bit down on his neck as he thrust hard and filled her. God! He felt so good!

They began to move together, cautiously at first, then lust took over, and they thrust frantically. She closed her legs around his back, drawing him deeper. His hand closed around her breast, and she screamed as he squeezed her nipple tight at the same time he thrust deep and hard.

"Come for me, Abbie," he breathed.

She nodded and moved faster; she wasn't sure that she'd be able to in this position, but he slid a hand between them and rested his thumb against her clit. That was all it took to push her over the edge. "Oh, oh, Ivan!"

"Yes!" His hips thrust harder and faster, driving her over the edge until her orgasm tore through her.

She let herself go, surrendering to the waves of pleasure that crashed through her. When she thought she couldn't go any higher, he found his release deep inside her, and he took her with him, spiraling them both higher and higher as she clung to him.

When they finally stilled, she rested her head on his shoulder for a moment. She wanted the feeling, the closeness, the intimacy to last. But reality returned all too soon. She closed her eyes. She'd just blown what could have been a friendship. He'd been amazing, but was it worth it? She half smiled—maybe; he might have been her best ever.

He shrugged his shoulder, making her lift her head. "Are you okay?"

She nodded.

"Disappointed?"

She shook her head rapidly. "I doubt you've ever disappointed a girl that way. Just disappointed in myself."

He frowned.

"Because I blew it."

"How?"

She shook her head. "It doesn't matter. I should go." She slid down from the counter, but when her feet hit the floor, he closed his arms around her.

"Please stay—for a while at least?"

"What for?"

He gave her a rueful smile. "To avoid the sewing machine and country music, if nothing else."

~ ~ ~

"Where's the powder room?"

He pointed to the hallway.

"I should clean up."

He watched her step inside, wondering if that meant she was getting herself ready to leave. He didn't wonder too long. He ran upstairs, hoping he'd be faster than she was. He was in such a hurry he almost caught himself in his zipper. He blew out a sigh and gave himself a stern look in the mirror. Idiot! What had he done? His hope for this evening had been to win her over—to prove to her that he was someone worth dating. Instead, he'd gone and proved her right. She'd told him he brought out the worst in her—and he'd done just that. He'd screwed her right there in the kitchen before she'd even finished her drink.

He caught himself smiling. It had been a dumb move, but he couldn't exactly regret it. He wanted more. She was amazing. He wanted to do it again, he wanted to get to know her body, get her naked, explore her. He shook his head. He needed to get back downstairs before she came out of the powder room and left. If he couldn't persuade her to stay and talk to him, he might never get the chance to explore their friendship—let alone her body.

He hurried back down the stairs and met her just as she was coming back into the hallway. He couldn't read her expression, but he knew it didn't bode well. He knew he had to say something, but he didn't know what. Instead, he went to her and slid his arms around her waist.

"Is it weird to say I'm sorry?"

She tensed, and for a moment, he thought she was going to push him away, but she relaxed and looked up into his eyes. "It's not weird at all. You're not as sorry as I am, though."

He tucked a strand of hair behind her ear. "Why, though, Abbs? What's so wrong with it?"

She pursed her lips. "I wasn't planning to stay and talk about it. I screwed up—I screwed you. That's not who I am anymore. I should go home. Go be the person I'm supposed to be now."

Even though she said she should go, she didn't make any attempt to move away from him. "You are the person you're supposed to be. You can't just change who you are."

"I guess. But I can make better choices."

He looked down into her eyes. "Do you really think I'm a bad choice?"

"No. You're a great choice—for someone. Someone who wants to hang out and fool around." She gave him a rueful smile. "Someone whose aim in life is to have some fun—and some great sex."

"Why can't that be your aim in life?"

She stepped away from him. "Because I've already had my fair share of fun and great sex."

"Better than we just had?" He couldn't help it. He needed to hear her say it.

She held his gaze for a long moment. "No."

He shrugged and gave her what he hoped was a cute smile. "So, why do we have to stop?"

"Because I have a different aim in life now. I need to settle down, start living the kind of life I should have been living all along. I need to meet a nice guy and get married and give my mom some grandkids while she's young enough to enjoy them."

"Why?" He knew he was pushing it, but he didn't understand. Her mom had made it obvious that she thought Abbie should go out with him. Hell, her mom was the reason she was here tonight. "She doesn't seem to have a problem with me."

Abbie blew out a sigh. "She just wants to see me happy. I want to make her happy."

"And you can't do both?"

"I'm hoping I can—but that's where it comes down to making better choices." She looked him in the eye. "I like you, Ivan." She smiled. "We're good together. It's going to be even harder to stay away from you now. But ..." she shook her head. "But we want different things in life."

He held her gaze. Part of him wanted to ask why she dismissed him as not being the kind of guy she wanted to be with. But he already knew the answer; he wasn't that kind of guy. At least, he never had been. He'd never been in a position where being in a relationship was an option. Sure, he dated, but nothing serious. Even though part of him wanted to, there was no point arguing with her.

He planted a kiss on her forehead. "I'm sorry you feel that way."

She looked up, her big brown eyes looked like melted chocolate. "Do you still want to be my friend?"

He tightened his arms around her waist. "Of course." He chuckled. "Are there any benefits involved?"

"No. There can't be. This was a mistake. I can't start dating a suitable guy and screwing you on the side. That wouldn't be right."

His heart hammered in his chest. The thought of her dating someone else made his arms tighten involuntarily around her. He didn't say anything—what could he say?

"So, do you want to finish that beer we barely started and hang out—as friends?"

"Yeah." It wasn't his favorite option for how to spend the rest of the evening—but it was better than her leaving, regretting what they'd done.

# Chapter Six

"Summer Lake Medical Center, how can I help you?"

"Hello. Is this Abbie?"

"Yes. Abbie speaking."

"Hi, Abbie. It's Neil."

Abbie frowned and looked around the waiting room. There were only a couple of people here. An older gentleman waiting to see Michael, and Kenzie who was waiting for Cassie. She knew full well they couldn't hear who was on the phone, but she still felt embarrassed.

"Hello. What can I do for you?" It sounded weird, and she knew it. It was the same voice she used when dealing with patients and their appointments, not the way she spoke to her friends.

"I ... I'm sorry to call you at work, but I didn't have your number. I wondered ... would you like to go out sometime?"

She closed her eyes. He was a sweet guy. He was exactly what she was looking for.

"I'm sorry. I didn't mean to be pushy. Can we forget that I called?"

"No!" She snapped out of it. The poor guy had obviously taken her silence as rejection. "I'm sorry. It's just busy in here. That'd be great. When?"

"Oh, err, Friday? Do you want to give me your number and I'll call you?"

"Friday's great." Kenzie was watching her, and for some reason, that made her nervous. "Can I take your number?" She didn't want Kenzie to hear her giving her number out.

She jotted Neil's down as he said it. "That's great, thanks. I'll give you a call."

"Okay." The poor guy sounded even more nervous now. He must wonder why she was speaking to him as though he was making a doctor's appointment.

"Okay, thanks. Bye." She hung up, feeling guilty. Neil deserved better than that. But she didn't want people to know she was taking personal calls at work. She didn't want Kenzie to know who she was talking to, and she didn't want to allow herself to stop and think about why she'd even said yes to Neil when she hadn't stopped thinking about Ivan since Sunday.

A shiver ran down her spine at the thought of him. It'd been a mistake, but one that she couldn't help reliving every time she got the chance. She'd thought about him in bed every night since—wishing that they'd made it as far as a bed.

Then Kenzie smiled at her, bringing her back to reality. Ivan was a no-go. They might have great sex, but that wasn't what she needed. She needed a nice guy to settle down with. Neil might just be that guy.

Mr. Santos came out of Michael's office and smiled at her as he left. A few moments later, Michael came out.

"Hey, Mr. Green. Come on in. Sorry, I'm running a little late." He turned to Abbie. "Everything okay out here?"

She nodded. She really needed to get a grip. He was only asking about the appointments. He didn't know anything about Neil or Ivan.

He held the door for Mr. Green to go into his office and then looked back at the waiting room. "Hey, Kenz. Are you guys still okay for tonight?"

"We are. We'll see you at six."

"Awesome. Thanks."

Michael closed the door behind him, and Kenzie got to her feet and came over to the desk.

"How's life with you?"

"Good, thanks. How about you?"

"Yep. All's well in my world."

Abbie almost asked why she was here, but just stopped herself in time. Patient confidentiality was one of the biggest requirements for this job. Sometimes it was hard because most of the patients were friends or acquaintances, and it was natural to ask how they were. "That's good."

"Are you coming to dinner with the girls on Thursday?"

"No. I can't this week."

"Why?" Kenzie wasn't the kind to let you off the hook.

"I have other plans."

Kenzie raised an eyebrow. "Are you seeing someone?"

Abbie smiled. "Maybe."

"Ooh!"

The door to Cassie's office opened, and Ann Hemming came out.

"I'll be going in in a minute," said Kenzie. "What time do you get off for lunch? Want to grab a bite with me?"

Abbie almost refused, but she liked Kenzie. "I get my break after your appointment. You're the last one this morning."

"Perfect!" Kenzie grinned at her. "See you in a little bit, then." She turned to Ann. "How are you? I haven't seen you for ages."

The older woman smiled. "I'm wonderful, thank you. How are you girls?"

"Good, thanks." Kenzie turned when Cassie's door opened, and she popped her head out. "Looks like that's me. It's good to see you, Mrs. Hemming. And I'll see you in a little bit, Abbs."

"Do you need another appointment?" Abbie asked once Kenzie had gone.

"Yes, please. One month from today."

Abbie set up her appointment in the computer and picked up an appointment card to write it out for her.

Mrs. Hemming laughed. "I know I'm an old fart, Abbie. But I don't need one of those. Can you email it to me so that it will sync with my calendar?"

"Oh! Sorry." The practice had a great electronic scheduling system, but she tended to assume that anyone over the age of fifty didn't use it.

"It's okay. I know you might think that we oldies are still in the stone age, but some of us keep up with technology."

"Of course."

"How's your mom doing?"

"She's okay, thanks. Doing better."

"That's good. I'm sure having you here has helped. How much longer do you plan to stay?"

Abbie frowned. "I'm back for good."

"Oh! I didn't realize. How do you feel about that?"

"It's my choice. I want to be here with her."

Mrs. Hemming frowned. "I know it's none of my business, but I'm sure your mom wants you to do what's best for you, not what you think is best for her."

Abbie forced herself to smile. She'd been hearing that a lot lately. "This is what's best for me."

"Well, good, then. I'll shut up and keep my nose out, shall I?" Mrs. Hemming gave her a friendly smile, and she felt bad.

"No! I know you mean well, you want to see me live my own life, but I can do that here as well as—or better than—anywhere else."

"I hope so. Your options are more limited here."

Abbie wondered whether she meant career options or boyfriend options. Either way, she was right, but it didn't matter. She had to be here to be with her mom, so the rest of the cards would have to fall as they may.

~ ~ ~

Ivan had to force himself to breathe when he realized that his jaw was clamped shut.

Neil hung up the phone and gave him a sheepish look. "Sorry. I didn't see you there. I don't usually make personal calls from work."

Ivan forced himself to smile though it felt more like a grimace. How could he hold anything against the guy? Neil was good people. He was quiet and reserved—words that people had told him about Abbie often enough. But apparently, he wasn't so shy that he wouldn't pick up the phone and ask a girl out. He wasn't to know that the girl he was asking was the same girl Ivan wanted to go out with—and stay in with.

"Are you mad at me?"

The silence had gone on for too long. "Mad? Not at all. Sorry. If anything, I feel like a shit for standing here listening to your call. I shouldn't have done that. I'm the one who should be sorry. You're right. I know you don't normally make personal calls. That's my only excuse. I didn't even think to give you some space." He straightened up from the doorway to Neil's office, where he'd been leaning. He'd come to talk to him but had stopped in his tracks when he'd heard him calling Abbie. His heart was still hammering in his chest.

"So, you're taking her out on Friday?"

Neil nodded slowly as a smile spread across his face. "She said yes! I can't believe it. I think I was only calling to put myself out of my misery. I haven't stopped thinking about her since we chatted at the Boathouse last weekend. I've kept imaging what it would be like to take her out. But she wouldn't be interested in someone like me. I know that. I figured if I called her and she turned me down then I'd have to stop thinking about it. But she said yes!"

Ivan forced another smile. If Neil were talking about any girl on earth other than Abbie, he would have been thrilled for him. "That's awesome," he managed to make himself say. "Where are you going?"

"I don't know. She said she'll call me. She's at work right now." His smile faded. "Do you think she will call? Or do you think that was a polite way to get out of it?"

Ivan's hopes soared. Maybe she wouldn't call? He had to pull himself together. "I'm sure she will. And if she doesn't call before Friday, at least you'll have your answer, right?"

Neil's face fell. "Yeah. I suppose so. Anyway. That's enough of my personal problems. What can I do for you?"

Ivan wanted to tell him that he could stay the hell away from Abbie, but instead, he racked his brain to remember why he'd come into his office in the first place. "Numbers." He nodded. That was it. "I need the cost projections for the first quarter of next year. Remember, I asked you what it'd look like if we ran two campaigns in tandem?"

"Sure. I'll email them to you right now."

"Thanks." Ivan turned to go, wishing that he'd simply emailed Neil to ask for them, then he wouldn't have overheard his phone call—wouldn't have witnessed him setting up his first date with Abbie.

"Ivan?"

He turned back. "Yeah?"

"This is going to sound pretty dorky, but can I ask you a favor?"

"Sure, anything." He regretted those words as soon as he'd spoken them.

"I'm going to drive out to the mall after work, is there any chance you'd want to come with me?"

"What do you need?" Ivan wanted to buy himself some time to think of a reason why he couldn't go.

Neil dropped his gaze. "Clothes. The kind I can wear on a date."

Ivan's heart sank. The guy wanted his advice on what to wear when he took Abbie out?

"It's okay. Forget I asked. I sound like a teenaged girl. I'll figure it out."

Neil looked so damned uncomfortable, Ivan couldn't help but feel bad for him. "It's okay. We can go as soon as we close up this afternoon if you want."

"Really? Thanks so much!"

Ivan nodded. "I'll be in my office if you need me." When he reached his office, he closed the door and slammed his fist against the wall. He hit it so much harder than he'd intended that he put a hole in the drywall. Damn.

He heard footsteps hurrying down the corridor.

"Are you okay in there?"

"I'm fine, Allie. Sorry about the noise." He opened the door and gave her an apologetic shrug.

"Are you sure?"

"I'm sure."

"Okay, then." She backed away, looking worried. The poor girl always seemed to look worried.

A little while later, he looked up from his computer when the buzzer on his desk sounded. He still hadn't gotten used to that thing. It made him jump every time.

He pressed the button. "What's up, Allie?"

"Mr. Davenport's here."

"Okay. I'll be right out."

He strode out to the little reception area where Allie manned the phones. She smiled at him and jerked her head to the parking lot, where Seymour Davenport was getting out of an SUV.

"I thought you'd want to be prepared."

Ivan grinned. "Thanks." She seemed to think that Mr. D was the big bad boss man and that they all had to be on their best behavior when he was around. Once upon a time, that would have been true, but he'd mellowed out a lot in the last few months.

He came in the door and smiled. "Ivan!"

"Mr. D! I didn't know you were back yet."

He grinned. "I came back early. I don't want to interrupt. I hope you're busy!"

Ivan laughed. "I am, but we're never too busy for you. Come on through."

"No, really, I don't want to interrupt. I just wanted to show my face and to ask if you're free on Friday night?"

Ivan frowned. He was. Unlike Neil.

"No problem if you're busy. It's just that Chris is going out with her sister, and I wondered if you'd like to get dinner together? You know, like the old days."

That made Ivan smile. The two of them had spent many evenings in the kitchen of Mr. D's Malibu house, having dinner together and shooting the breeze. Things were different now, and they hadn't done anything like that since they came to Summer Lake. "I'd love to."

"You don't have other plans? I'd understand if you've found yourself a nice young lady."

"Nope."

Mr. D raised an eyebrow. "Oh, dear. That sounds like there's a story behind it."

Ivan shrugged.

"Do you want to meet at the Boathouse at seven on Friday, and you can tell me all about it?"

Hell, no! That was the last place Ivan wanted to go. He couldn't imagine sitting there watching Abbie and Neil. "How about you come over to the house? I can throw us something together—or we can order out."

Mr. D laughed. "We'll order out. It'll be better than the Boathouse anyway. It'll be loud with the band."

It'd be too distracting with Abbie there on a date, too. "Yeah."

"And I want to see how you're settling in."

Ivan didn't want to tell him that the house was still the same as the day he'd moved in. He'd find out for himself on Friday.

~ ~ ~

"How long do you have, and where do you want to go?" asked Kenzie.

"I have an hour, and we can go wherever you like. Do you want to try the bakery?"

Kenzie laughed. "Mind-reader. I spend most of my life at the Boathouse, I prefer to go elsewhere when I get the chance."

"Hey, ladies!" April, who worked with Renée, greeted them with a smile. "Grab a table. I'll be right over."

They chose a table by the window, and Kenzie checked her watch.

"Are you short on time?" asked Abbie.

Kenzie laughed. "No. If you want to know the truth, I was figuring out how long I have to interrogate you before you have to get back."

"Interrogate me? About what?"

"About everything. I want to know your story."

Abbie's heart sank. She didn't want to tell her story. She wished that people who did know it would forget it. Kenzie was one of the newcomers who didn't know it, and Abbie would rather it stayed that way. "There's not much to tell."

Kenzie gave her a shrewd look. "More like not much that you want to tell. You can't bullshit a bullshitter, sugar. I have a feeling that you and I have more in common than you might think."

"What can I get you, girls?"

Abbie was relieved when April came to take their order. Once she'd gone, Kenzie smiled. "Come on. What's the deal with you? You make out like you're this Miss Goody Two-shoes, but that's not who you are. I asked Michael, and he wouldn't tell me anything."

Abbie was glad that Michael respected her privacy—despite the fact that Kenzie was his sister-in-law and could be very persuasive.

"What are you hiding?"

"I'm not hiding anything. I just want a fresh start. I want to be a whole new person, and if I'm going to do that, then I don't need to bring the past with me."

"True. Tell me to butt out if you want. I'm just curious. You feel like a kindred spirit, yet you …" She smiled. "Sorry. I think I was kind of hoping that you'd turn out to be like me."

Abbie had to smile. "You said we might have more in common than I realize, what do you mean?"

"Don't take it wrong if I'm way off the mark, but before I came here, I was a total screw up. People here have been good to me. I fell on my feet. Between Ben giving me a job and Michael and his family taking me in along with Megan, and of course, meeting Chase, I've made good. But before I came up here …" She shrugged. "I didn't live the same kind of life I do now."

Abbie nodded. "You had it rough?"

"I made it rough on myself by the way I was living—the choices I made."

"That's definitely something we have in common then."

"Want to tell me about it?"

Abbie looked around. There was no one sitting close by. "You know about my dad?"

"Yeah. I'm sorry."

"Not as sorry as I am. I left here after high school—with a boy. We moved to LA. It didn't last long. I stayed there and ..." She smiled. "If I say that I didn't live the same kind of life I do now, would that tell you what you need to know?"

"Yeah. You partied hard, screwed around, had a lot of fun, and made some bad decisions?"

"That about sums it up."

April came back with their sandwiches. "Here you go. I didn't know the two of you were friends. Seems like everyone knows everyone around here."

Kenzie smiled at her. "Yeah, we go way back, Abbie and me."

"I'll leave you to catch up then."

"Mind if I ask you something?"

"You can ask. I'm not promising that I'll answer."

"Why the act now?"

"It's not an act. I don't want to be that girl anymore."

Kenzie made a face. "You don't get to be someone else. You're still you."

"Are you still the same person?"

"Hell, yeah, I am! I just enjoy different things now. I got around good people and found out that I enjoy a different life. I thought it'd be boring here, but I have more fun here than I ever did before—and a lot less trouble too." She smiled. "You just need to get around the right kind of people."

"I'm working on that."

"What do you mean?"

Abbie wasn't sure that she wanted to tell her, but it was a relief to finally talk to someone who understood where she was coming from and could relate to where she wanted to go.

"Have you met someone?"

Abbie nodded.

"It's Ivan, isn't it? Don't tell Chase, but whoa, that man is hot!"

"No!" Abbie shook her head rapidly. "Not Ivan! I have a date on Friday with Neil."

Kenzie made a face. "Neil? Who the hell is Neil? I can tell you for nothing that he's not as hot as Ivan."

Abbie sighed. "Exactly. That's why I'm going out with Neil."

"What? That doesn't make any sense at all. Ivan's hot—and he's hot for you. Neil is—who the hell is Neil? Help me out with that one first."

"He's an accountant."

"Oh, good Lord!"

Abbie had to laugh. "He's very sweet."

"Umm, sweet accountant or hot Ivan. I know which one I'd choose. I know which one you'd choose."

"You obviously don't because I'm choosing Neil."

"Why?"

"I thought you understood? Ivan's the kind of guy I've always been with—hot, fun, sweet, totally unreliable. No good for me. Neil is the kind of guy the new Abbie wants to be with."

"Boring?"

"He's not boring!"

"Maybe. I can't judge the guy. I don't know him. But that in itself tells you something. I know everyone in this town—everyone who has a life and comes out to the Boathouse even occasionally."

"He was there last weekend."

"Oh! That was the dude you were talking to?"

Abbie nodded.

"While Ivan was watching you like a hawk."

"He was?"

"Yup. I think you're crazy. You should go out with Ivan instead."

"No."

Kenzie smirked. "If I were in your shoes, at least go home with Ivan."

Abbie dropped her gaze.

"You did, didn't you?!"

"I'm not proud of it."

Kenzie waved a hand at her. "Was it mind-blowing?"

Abbie had to smile. "Yes. It was, if you must know."

"You are one crazy, mixed-up kid."

"That's the point. I'm trying to grow up and not be a kid. I'm trying to make the sensible choice."

"I'm not going to try to talk you out of it. You get to make your own choices, but I'll be here if you want a friend—if you need someone to talk to when you figure out what a mess you're making of things."

"That's exactly the same thing Ivan said."

"Damn, girl. So, you told him, and he's understanding about it?"

"Yeah, I suppose he is."

"And you still don't think he's the sensible choice? If you ask me, you're a fool. But I've got your back. Just don't hurt this Neil guy in the process. Okay?"

That was something she hadn't even considered. She'd been so busy trying to figure out what she wanted and how to build the kind of life that she thought she should be living that she hadn't stopped to think whether her ideal guy might get hurt in the process.

Kenzie gave her a shrewd look. "Be careful. If anything, you need to be as honest with him as it sounds like you've been with Ivan. It's only fair."

Abbie pursed her lips. "I'm not sure he'd be so understanding."

"That's kind of my point!"

# Chapter Seven

Ivan looked around the living room. He wondered if Mr. D would tell him the same thing that Colt had—that he should do something to make this place look more like a home. He hoped not, because if Mr. D said it, he'd feel like he had to do something, and he had no idea what that something might be.

He checked the clock. It was almost seven-thirty. He couldn't help but wonder what Abbie was doing right now. Was she getting ready? Was she in the shower? No. He couldn't let his mind go there.

Much as he wished he didn't, he knew that Neil would be going to pick her up at eight. He felt bad. He'd kept his word and gone out to the mall with Neil to help him find something to wear. They'd found him a pair of jeans and a black pullover that looked good on him. In his own words, he looked more like Ivan than a stuffy accountant.

He blew out a sigh. Maybe he was doing Abbie a favor. She said she wanted to be with someone like Neil, and her actions had proved that she enjoyed being with someone who looked like him. Maybe this way she'd end up with the best of both worlds.

He started at the sound of the doorbell. Mr. D was always ten minutes early—it wasn't likely he was here a whole half hour early.

He was, though. "I hope you don't mind?" he asked when Ivan opened the door. "Chris went out half an hour ago, and I didn't know what else to do with myself."

Ivan grinned. "I don't mind at all. Come on in." He led him through to the kitchen. "What are you drinking?"

"I'll take a beer, thanks."

"I have a bottle of your bourbon if you want that—don't think you're stuck with beer just because I'm a heathen."

He laughed. "Thanks. But I'd like a beer. I've learned to enjoy it."

"Okay, then." Ivan got two bottles from the fridge. "Do you want a glass?"

"No, thanks." Mr. D popped the top off his with a grin. "They really do taste better out of the bottle."

Ivan laughed. "You've come a long way in the last couple of years."

"I have. But what about you? Your life has changed just as much as mine has lately. I hope it's all for the better?"

Ivan thought about it. He was enjoying life at the lake. It suited him. He'd made new friends. He even felt like part of the community. If it weren't for Abbie—for the fact that he couldn't be with Abbie—he'd be happy. He nodded.

Mr. D frowned. "I have to be honest; I was hoping for a more enthusiastic response."

"Sorry. Everything's great. I'm happy here."

"But?"

"But nothing. It's all good."

Mr. D gave him a skeptical look. "Something's not right. I can tell. Is it a girl?"

Ivan blew out a sigh. "Kind of. It's more that it's not a girl."

"What, that there isn't a girl? Or there is one, and it's not happening between the two of you."

"That. It's not happening. It can't happen."

"I'm sorry. Why not?"

"Because she wants to settle down, get married, and have kids with a suitable, reliable kind of guy."

"And you don't?"

"It doesn't matter. She doesn't think I'm suitable."

"Why not? You're a catch—I would have thought. You have a great job if I do say so myself. You have a very bright future. You have a lovely home." He looked around. "Though you might want to do something about making it feel like yours."

"It's not any of that. She just …" He blew out a sigh. "If you want to know the truth, she's out with Neil tonight. He's the kind of suitable she's looking for."

"Ah. Well, it seems to me that the kind of girl who'd go for Neil isn't the kind of girl you'd go for."

"I know. She's trying to be someone she's not."

"Why?"

"To make up for mistakes she's made in the past."

"Well, I hate to say it, Ivan, but it sounds like she's not worth it. Not yet anyway."

Ivan had to bite back the anger that surged up out of nowhere. "She is."

Mr. D held up his hand. "All I'm saying is that it sounds as though she has some things to figure out before she'd be as ready for a relationship as you are."

Ivan frowned. "I am?"

"Yes! It wouldn't bother you this much if you weren't. Would it?"

"I guess not."

"Give her some time. And while you're waiting, it might be worth your while to figure out what you really want."

"It's not often you're wrong, but you're right again." Ivan was a little taken aback by Mr. D's assumption that he was ready for a real relationship. The weirdest part about it was that he had a feeling he was right.

"Did you do anything about ordering dinner?"

"Not yet. I was waiting to see what you wanted."

"Do you want to go over to the Boathouse?"

"No! That's where Abbie and Neil are."

"Ah. Okay then. Shall we call Giuseppe's for a pizza?"

"Yeah, that'd be better."

~ ~ ~

Abbie looked herself over in the mirror. She didn't want to look too good. No, that wasn't right. She did want to look good—but good in Neil's eyes was different than her version. Nothing too tight, nothing too short. Not that she wore anything short and tight anymore anyway. She pulled on a dress. It was okay. The V-neck wasn't too low. The sleeves were three-quarter length, and it fell to mid-calf. She'd bought it to attend a christening last winter. She looked like a respectable young woman. That made her laugh. She *was* a respectable young woman. But then, so was Kenzie—and she wouldn't be caught dead in this dress!

Once her makeup was done—the same as she did it for work—she went downstairs.

Her mom did a double take when she saw her. "What …?"

"What, what?"

"What are you wearing? Are you going on a date or going to church?"

Abbie made a face. "I'm going on a date. I told you. With Neil."

"I know what you said, but what are you wearing?"

"I take it you don't like it?"

"I didn't say that. I'm sorry, sweetie. It's just different from what you normally wear to go out."

"It's not that different. I thought you'd like it."

Her mom pursed her lips. "Abbie, we need to have a chat. I know you've been trying so hard to do things differently since you came back. And I won't argue with you that you used to be a bit wild. But this …? You're going to the opposite extreme. I don't want you dressing up like some old fuddy-duddy. It's not who you are."

Abbie stared at her. She wanted to be angry, wanted to tell her mom that she was making these changes for her—so she could proud of her. She took a deep breath. The last thing she wanted to do was fight. So, instead, she gave a little laugh. "Fuddy-duddy? What's one of those? I've never heard that before. For a second there I wondered what you were going to say."

Her mom laughed. "Don't worry. I'm too much of a lady to say some old fucker, but it's probably what your dad would have said."

This time Abbie's laugh was genuine. "You're right. I can hear him." Her laughter caught in her throat as tears welled up in her eyes. "I wish he was still here."

Her mom nodded, her eyes glistening. "So do I. And if he were, he'd tell you to stop this. He'd want you to keep being you, Abbie."

"I am being me, Mom. Just a better version."

"There was nothing wrong with the old version."

Abbie pursed her lips. "This isn't the time to get into it, Mom."

"I know, but one day soon, we need to. What time's Ivan picking you up?"

"Ivan?" Her heart raced at the mention of his name. She'd kept pushing him out of her thoughts all week. Just when she needed it least, her mom was bringing him up. "I'm going out with Neil. I told you."

"Sorry. You did. I like Ivan."

"You'll like Neil, too. Did I tell you he's an accountant?"

"Pft. Only about twelve times, though why you think that would make me like him, I have no idea."

"Well, it's because he has a good job. He's responsible."

"So? Is he fun? Does he give you butterflies?"

"I don't know yet. I'm hoping to find that out tonight." She wasn't about to admit that when she'd chatted with him at the Boathouse last weekend, the conversation had been more stilted than fun.

The doorbell rang, and they stared at each other. Abbie wasn't ready for this.

"You'd better get that."

Typical. When she needed a minute to prepare herself, her mom sent her to open the door. Last weekend she'd been lurking by it ready to let Ivan in herself.

She hurried to the door and had to stop herself from gasping when she opened it.

"Hi, Abbie."

Neil presented her with a bunch of flowers, but it wasn't those that took her breath away. It was like some weird joke the universe was playing on her. He was dressed like Ivan. He looked like he was trying to be Ivan, in dark jeans and a black pullover with a black leather jacket, which, if she didn't know better, she would say was Ivan's.

"Hi. Thank you! I'm sorry. Just let me get my coat." She was so flustered she left him standing on the doorstep while she went back in.

Her mom eyed the flowers then made her way to the door. "Come on in."

Abbie rolled her eyes and took the flowers to the kitchen. When she came back to the living room, her mom was smiling, and Neil was looking decidedly uncomfortable.

"It's nice to meet you, Neil. I don't think we've met before, have we? Are you new to the lake?"

"It's nice to meet you, too, Mrs. ..."

"Mrs. Parsons."

Abbie didn't miss that. She'd told Ivan he could call her Nina.

"I've been here for a couple of months now. I moved here from San Francisco."

"Oh, my. What brought you to the boonies from the big city?"

"A job. I've always worked for non-profits, and I was fortunate to be offered a position working for Seymour Davenport when he set up his office here. So far, I'm enjoying small-town life."

Abbie's heart thudded to a halt. He worked for Seymour Davenport? That meant he worked with Ivan. Did that have anything to do with the way he was dressed? Oh. God! Had Ivan dressed him for his date? Did Ivan know about tonight?

She sucked in a deep breath. What did it matter? It didn't. Or … it might. Neil couldn't know about her and Ivan. No one could know. But especially not Neil.

She forced herself to come back to reality. Her mom was saying something about not everyone being cut out for small-town life. It was time to go. She zipped up her coat and smiled at Neil.

"Are you ready?"

"Yes. It was nice to meet you, Mrs. Parsons."

"And you. Have a nice time."

"Thank you."

Abbie bundled him out of the door as fast as she could.

Once they were out on the street, he smiled nervously at her.

She smiled back. It didn't look like he was going to say anything. She looked around, wondering which was his car.

"I thought we could walk since it's not far."

"Oh. Okay." She couldn't help remembering that Ivan had driven here—so that she wouldn't have to freeze her ass off on the way home. And he'd driven her home after their evening together. The little voice in her head added that he'd driven it home during their evening, too.

They started walking in silence. Abbie racked her brain for something to say. The poor guy was obviously nervous. It'd be down to her to break the ice.

"What did you do in San Francisco?"

"Much the same as I do here. I worked for a non-profit."

"What kind of charity was that?"

"It supports homeless vets. It does a lot of good work."

"That's good."

Silence fell between them again. She wanted to talk to him, but she couldn't think of anything to say. Other than the fact that she desperately wanted to ask him if Ivan had dressed him for this date.

"Are you enjoying working here? Are the people nice?"

He smiled. "It's a very small office. There's only half a dozen of us—though we will be expanding next year. I don't tend to socialize much at work." He shot a quick glance at her. "I should probably admit that I didn't need to add the words *at work* to the end of that sentence."

Aww. She felt bad. She wanted to say something to set him at ease, but he hurried on.

"But I do like my coworkers. They're a mix of locals and newcomers. The guy who runs the office has worked for Mr. Davenport for several years. He was his chauffeur before, but he's a great leader in the office."

"Do you like him?"

"I do. I'm not sure I'm his kind of person. But he's been kind to me. You could say he's the closest thing to a friend I've made here yet."

"That's good."

"It is."

The silence lengthened as they walked on. Abbie was glad that Ivan had been good to Neil. She frowned as a thought struck her. "Has he been good to you since you first arrived?"

"Ivan? Yes. He has. He helped me get settled in."

"That's good. The people you work with make a big difference in your life."

"Do you work with good people?"

She smiled. He was finally asking questions instead of just answering them. "I do. I work for two doctors, and they're good people." Now that she came to think about it, they'd both been good to her, too.

# Chapter Eight

The Boathouse was busy, as it always was on the weekend, but they found an empty high-top table. It was right in the back near the bathrooms, but at least it was quieter back here. Abbie hoped that fewer people would see them, too.

"I'll go and get us a drink," said Neil. "What would you like?"

"A white wine, please."

"What kind?"

She didn't usually drink wine. She thought it would sound better to him than asking for a beer. She didn't know what kinds there might be. "Err, a Chardonnay, please." She knew her mom drank that sometimes.

He nodded, and she watched him make his way to the bar. She had a feeling it would be a while before he returned. The bar was three deep, and he wasn't the kind of guy who would push his way through to get served. She sighed as she watched him stand there. He was sweet enough. Maybe once he had a drink he'd relax enough to get talking properly. Maybe there'd be more of a spark between them then.

Her mom's voice echoed in her mind. *Does he give you butterflies?* She made a face. So far, he didn't even give her caterpillars!

"Hey! What are you doing sitting back here, making funny faces to yourself? Come and join us. Everyone's sitting over there."

She looked up at Roxy, who was pointing to a table by the dance floor. "That's okay, thanks. I'm not by myself."

Roxy looked at the empty seat opposite her and raised an eyebrow.

"He's gone to the bar."

"Oh! Want to tell me who he is?"

"Neil."

Roxy frowned. "Who's Neil? I was sure you were going to say Ivan. I've been waiting to hear that the two of you got together."

Abbie decided she'd do better to avoid the second half of the question and only focus on the first. "Neil's fairly new in town. He's an accountant. He works for Seymour Davenport."

"Oh. So, you mean he works with Ivan? Did he introduce you?"

"No." Abbie blew out a sigh. "Why does everyone seem to think there's something between Ivan and me?"

Roxy laughed. "Because we have eyes in our heads. There's something about the way you look at each other. Something that crackles in the air when you get within ten feet of each other. It's hard to miss. You can't tell me you don't know it."

Abbie wanted to tell her exactly that, but for all her faults, she wasn't a liar. "I can't tell you that, no. But I can tell you that nothing's going to happen between us. It can't."

"Why not?"

"Because we're not right for each other."

Roxy smiled. "I thought that about Logan and me. I was wrong, though."

At that moment, her fiancé Logan came to stand by her side. He slung an arm around her shoulders and dropped a kiss on her lips. "There you are. I wondered if you fell down the toilet or something. I was coming to rescue you."

Roxy laughed, and Abbie couldn't help but smile at the way she pushed at his arm. "I haven't been gone that long. I found Abbie sitting here by herself."

"You should come sit with us." Logan met her gaze. Before he and Roxy had gotten together, Abbie had known that he would have taken her to bed any time she wanted to go. They'd gone to high school together, and he'd been like a male version of herself. These days he was a very different character, though.

"I'm fine, thanks. I'm with someone. He's at the bar."

"Oh." Logan raised his eyebrows. "Anyone we know? Should we stick around to say hi or skedaddle before he gets back?"

Abbie shrugged. "Stick around if you want."

"It's not Ivan, though," said Roxy.

Logan looked surprised. "Who is it, then?"

Abbie rolled her eyes. "It's Neil."

Logan laughed. "Neil, the mild-mannered accountant? You're not serious? You and Neil?"

She gave him an evil look, and Roxy slapped his arm.

Abbie spotted Neil on his way back with their drinks. "Be nice to him, Logan. Here he comes."

He set the drinks down on the table and smiled at them all. "Sorry, that took a while."

Logan grinned at him. "Yeah, you need to elbow your way through when it's busy like this."

Abbie narrowed her eyes at him, but he gave her an innocent smile.

Roxy held her hand out to Neil. "I don't think we've ever been introduced. I'm Roxy. It's nice to meet you."

"You, too. I'm Neil."

Abbie closed her eyes briefly when she saw Kenzie coming toward them. That was all she needed. Kenzie didn't even need to elbow people aside; the crowd parted before her. The regulars knew not to get in her way, and visitors soon learned.

"Abbie! So, this is your hot date?"

Neil smiled at her. "I'm her date, at least."

Kenzie put a hand on his arm. "It's all in the eye of the beholder, sugar. But I thought you were beholding Merry, who works with Megan?"

Abbie frowned. She had no idea what Kenzie was up to—or who Merry was.

Poor Neil's cheeks flamed bright red. "I ... I ..."

Kenzie winked at him. "It's okay. I won't tell her you were out with our Abbie."

Abbie looked at Neil.

"There's no reason I shouldn't be here with you. Merry and I aren't seeing each other or anything."

"Did she turn you down, or did you never get up the balls to ask her?"

Abbie wanted to tell Kenzie to shut up. She shouldn't pick on him like that.

Neil looked stricken. Roxy and Logan looked uncomfortable, too.

Kenzie grinned around them all. "You know me. I just like to see everyone happy."

"You've got a funny way of going about it," said Abbie. "Looks to me like you're making all of us unhappy. Or at least uncomfortable."

"I'm uncomfortable enough to say that we're out of here," said Roxy. She took hold of Logan's hand. "We'll catch you later, Abbie."

Abbie watched them go, then looked back at Neil and Kenzie.

"Does one of you want to tell me what's going on?"

Kenzie looked at Neil, and he, in turn, looked at Abbie. "I'm sorry. I don't know what it's got to do with Kenzie. I have had a bit of a crush on Merry who works at the library, but there's no chance anything's going to happen between us. Then I met you, and well … you're beautiful, and we got along quite well, and …" he shrugged. "I wanted to test myself. I didn't think I'd have the nerve to ask you out, but I did. I certainly didn't think that you'd say yes—but you did, and so here we are."

"But you'd rather be here with Merry, right?" asked Kenzie.

Abbie shot daggers at her, but she just shrugged.

Neil looked at his feet and them up at them both. The poor guy looked like he wanted the floor to open up and swallow him.

Abbie was a little disappointed that he didn't speak—that he didn't deny what Kenzie was saying.

Kenzie smiled at him, and when she spoke again, her voice was much gentler. "I'm not doing this just to be a bitch. I know it's none of my business, but I can't help sticking my nose in. I don't like seeing you here together when I know that you'd both rather be somewhere else."

Abbie looked at Neil. "Is that true?"

He nodded slowly. "I find you very attractive, Abbie. But you have to admit there isn't anything going on between us, is there? There's no spark."

She smiled. "I was hoping that one might develop."

He smiled back at her. "I was, too, but let's face it. I'm not your kind of guy, and you're not my kind of girl."

Abbie knew he was right. Even though it did sting a little.

Kenzie put a hand on Neil's shoulder. "Please don't hate me. I promise I'll do anything I can to help you move things along with Merry. I just couldn't watch the two of you waste each other's time."

"I don't hate you. I appreciate it."

"Okay. Well, now I've ruined your night, I'd better get back to work!"

Abbie watched her leave, then turned back to Neil. "Do you want to call it a night?"

He held up his glass. "I think I need to drink this first."

She chuckled and picked up her wine. "Me, too." She took a sip. "Do you mind if I ask why you think there's no chance between you and Merry?"

He blew out a sigh. "She's not very sociable."

"So, she won't go out with you?"

"She doesn't go out much at all."

"Have you even asked her?"

He shook his head.

"So, ask her! You didn't think I'd say yes, but I did. Maybe she will, too."

"Maybe."

Abbie smiled. "I'll help if you want. Go in the library and talk you up."

He smiled back. "You would? Why?"

"Because I'd like to see you get what you want. And now I know that isn't me."

"Don't say it like that. That makes it sound as though you wanted something to develop between us."

She held his gaze for a long moment. "I thought I did."

He shook his head. "We're too different, Abbie. And we both know it. Look at you, you're wearing a dress that you wouldn't normally wear. I got a friend to go shopping with me so that I might look as cool as he does. I even went back and bought a jacket because it's like the one he wears. Just to go out on one date. We've both tried to dress like someone we're not—to change who we are. That should tell us all we need to know. We'd make each other miserable. I don't know much about relationships, but I do know that you need to be true to yourself and find someone who likes you for what you are inside. You can't pretend to be someone else, and if you do, it'll make you unhappy."

She raised her glass to him. "A lot of people have tried to tell me that same thing lately, and for some reason, you're the one who finally managed to get it through my thick skull. Thanks, Neil."

He raised his glass and tapped it against hers. "You're welcome—and thank you, too, for helping me figure it out. I was so excited that you said yes, but ever since you did, I've been wishing that I'd had the nerve to ask Merry instead."

He drained his glass. "I think I'd like to leave now. This really isn't my scene. Would you like me to walk you home?"

"No. Thanks. I might stay awhile."

He got down from his stool and pulled that leather jacket on. "I'll see you around, I guess."

"You'll do more than that. I'll give you a call in the week and see if you've made any progress with Merry. If you haven't, I might just pay a visit to the library and put in a good word for you."

He chuckled. "I'm not sure I'm ready for that kind of scheming. But I appreciate the thought." He leaned in and planted a kiss on her cheek. "You take care, Abbie."

"You, too, Neil. I'll see you soon."

~ ~ ~

Ivan looked at the clock. It was only ten-thirty. It'd been a good evening with Mr. D. They hadn't hung out like that in a long time. It'd been good to catch up. Good to solidify their new relationship. Things had changed between them since they'd come to Summer Lake. Before there had been no question that Mr. D was the employer and he was the employee—Ivan had even told Mr. D at one point that he only saw him as the help. That had never been true, and now they had a real friendship as well as a working relationship. When Mr. D had offered him the opportunity to run the office here, he'd expected that he'd still be something of a minion, but that wasn't the case at all. He pretty much ran the show, and Mr. D trusted him to do so.

He took a fresh beer from the fridge and went to stand in front of the windows that looked out on the lake. The moon was already high in the sky, and it cast a silver sheen on the water. He might have said it looked romantic—if he were given to such thoughts. Generally, he wasn't, but tonight he couldn't help but wish that Abbie was here to see the moonlight. They could take a walk down by the water's edge.

He took a slug of his beer. They wouldn't do that, not tonight or any other night. Tonight, she was out with Neil. He wondered what they were doing at this very moment. Were they talking, laughing? Was she flicking her hair over her shoulders in the same flirty way she had when she was talking to Neil last weekend? Was Neil sitting there—in the clothes that Ivan had picked out for him—thinking what a lucky son of a bitch he was? He sighed. Probably. And if he wasn't, then he was an idiot.

He started to pace. It was too early to go to bed. He needed to do something, something more than moping around here. He set his beer down on the island and went to get his coat. He wasn't going to go for a romantic walk on the shore by himself, but he could take a power walk through town and hopefully, burn off some of his pent-up energy and frustration before he turned in for the night.

He strode down Main Street toward the resort. He was hardly going to go to the Boathouse, but he could cut through a couple of streets before he reached the square. The last thing he wanted was to see Abbie walking hand in hand with Neil— or to run into any of his friends who might invite him to come and listen to the band for a while.

He passed the first street he could have turned down and walked on toward the second. He told himself that he was taking the shortest route to the town center, but part of him knew that he was taking the route that took him closer to where Abbie was.

He cocked his head to one side as he came into view of the square. A lone figure was walking across, cutting through the parked cars. He hoped she was heading toward the line of taxis. Not only was it too damned cold for anyone with any sense to be out walking, but he didn't like the idea of a woman walking home alone. Especially not when that woman looked a lot like … was it? It couldn't be. She had long dark hair, but she was dressed more like a middle-aged … He squinted. It sure as hell looked like Abbie, but maybe it was her mom?

He hurried forward to get a better look. Maybe he was just imagining things.

The woman pulled her coat tighter around her and walked past the line of cabs. Now he really wanted to know who it was. She cut down the street he'd planned to take, and he lengthened his stride to follow her. Whoever she was, he needed to make sure she got home safely.

She looked back over her shoulder, and his heart raced. It was her. "Abbie!"

She stopped and turned around, frowning when she recognized him. "What are you doing here?"

"I could ask you the same thing. Why are you walking home alone?" He caught up to her and stopped a few yards away. "Where's Neil?"

She scowled. "You mean, where's your little Ivan doll who you dressed up just like you?"

He blew out a sigh. "What do you think I should have done, turned him down when he asked me to help him find something to wear on his date?"

She pursed her lips.

"Well?" She was obviously mad at him, and in a way, he couldn't blame her. He'd felt like an asshole when Neil had wanted to get clothes like his.

"I don't know. I get it, I suppose. Did you know who his date was with?"

"I sure did. Can you imagine how that made me feel?"

She took a step toward him. "No. Tell me?"

That took him by surprise. He didn't want to tell her. Why would he? "Where is he?" He changed the subject instead.

"He went home a couple of hours ago."

Ivan bit back a smile. "Why?"

"Because, apparently, I'm not his type."

"Jesus! What is he, crazy?"

The hint of a smile hovered on her lips. "Actually, I think he's pretty smart. He told me that we shouldn't pretend to be someone we're not and that if we do, we'll only make ourselves and the people around us miserable."

"So, when he tells you, it's smart, but when I told you the exact same thing, you told me to mind my own business."

She shrugged. "I suppose it gets through when you hear it from someone who doesn't matter."

Ivan unclenched his jaw. He'd been angry that she'd listen to Neil and not to him, but what did she mean?

She smiled.

"What are you saying?"

"I'm saying you were right, and I'm sorry."

His heart started to race. "Before I screw this up, explain it to me? What was I right about?"

"You're right that I shouldn't try to be someone I'm not."

He nodded. That was good, but it didn't mean she saw him any differently than she had before. He waited.

"And you were right that you and me—us—we're, we might … maybe …"

He took a step closer, hoping that she was saying what he thought she was. She was struggling, and he didn't want to put it all on her. He smiled. "Are you saying that I might have a chance?"

She nodded.

He held his arms out to her, and she stepped into them. He wanted to kiss her, but that didn't seem right. A girl shouldn't start her night on a date with one guy and end up going home with another. He knew that between the two of them, what started as kissing would only ever lead to the bedroom.

Instead, he hugged her to his chest. "I'm not as bad as you seem to think I am, Abbie."

"I never thought you were bad. I just know that we're the same kind of animal. We're about the good times, not about the long term. I thought I needed to get straight to the long-term stuff, but even my mom says I should just figure out how to be me—that I don't need to hurry up and settle down just yet."

"What are you saying?"

"That maybe we can have some good times together. Hang out, go out, you know."

He nodded and dropped a kiss on top of her head. He did know what she meant. What he didn't know was how to tell her that he might want to explore more than that—the long-term stuff, as she called it. And he sure as hell didn't know how to ask if she'd be interested in that with him. "I'd like that."

She looked up at him. "I don't mean that I want to go home with you tonight. That wouldn't be right."

He smiled. "I can't say I don't want you to, but it wouldn't feel right to me either. Do you still need help with a Christmas tree?"

"Huh?"

"I was still planning on making a nuisance of myself and coming over this weekend. I figured your mom would accept my help even if you don't want it."

She smiled. "Well, now you know that I do, too."

"Okay. I'll call you tomorrow, then. For now, let's get you home."

When they reached her house, she unlatched the gate and looked up at him. "Thanks, Ivan. I feel like I don't deserve you being so understanding."

He reached up and touched her cheek. "You deserve the world, Abbie. Don't ever tell yourself otherwise."

He wanted to kiss her, but he stepped away instead. He'd see her tomorrow, and he'd rather they started whatever this was going to be on a new day—not on the tail-end of her failed date with someone else.

"Goodnight. I'll call you tomorrow."

She stood on her tiptoes and planted a sweet little peck on his cheek. "I'll look forward to it."

# Chapter Nine

Abbie woke up early on Saturday morning. She should be working today, but Mrs. Evans had asked if she could swap. Abbie was happy to let her. Saturday mornings at the practice always meant kids running around the waiting room. It often meant snotty kids, too. She wasn't a fan.

She snuggled deeper under the duvet. It wasn't seven yet—it wouldn't even get light for over an hour. Usually, she liked to stay in bed on these dark mornings when she got the chance, but this morning she couldn't settle back down. She was too excited.

Today, Ivan was going to call her. He was going to help her find a Christmas tree for her mom. And … and she didn't know what else, but she hoped it would involve going to his place and getting to know each other better. He might not be interested in settling down—he'd told her that upfront that first night that they'd had a drink together. But he was interested in dating—and everything that went with it. That was enough. It'd have to be.

It was funny really that Neil was the one who'd managed to make her see what everyone else had been telling her. She'd believed all this time that she needed to become someone else.

Maybe it was because she'd actually tried to be someone else with him and had seen for herself just how awkward and uncomfortable it was. They hadn't even gotten started on their date before it had become apparent that it wouldn't work. No way would she be able to live her whole life that way.

She rolled over and looked out the window into the darkness. She'd been prepared to set out on a path toward marriage and domestic bliss, but she could admit now that it would be more like a nightmare.

Ivan was smarter than she was. He wasn't looking to settle down. She'd told him last night that they were the same kind of animal. He just knew himself better than she did. He knew that he wasn't cut out for that kind of life. She frowned. Or maybe he just didn't see himself living that way with her—he'd told her outright that he wasn't going to marry her and produce offspring. She sighed. She shouldn't want him to either. That wasn't who he was—and he knew it.

She sat up. She shouldn't be lying here thinking about what could never happen between her and Ivan. She should get her ass out of bed and start the day—get excited about what was going to happen. They'd have fun, she knew that. And if she had to put money on it, she'd bet that they'd have sex, too. A shiver ran down her spine at the thought.

Last weekend in his kitchen had been amazing, but it had been quick and guilt-ridden, too. She'd felt like she shouldn't be doing it. Now, she saw no reason why not. She wasn't going back to her old ways. She wasn't going to be screwing around. She hugged her knees to her chest. She was just going to be screwing Ivan—as hard and as often as they could.

She went downstairs and started making coffee. Her mom wasn't up yet, and she loved it when the coffee was ready before she was.

She went and opened the curtains in the dining room and looked out at the back yard. "Holy shit!"

It had snowed! There was maybe a couple of inches on the ground. She hadn't expected that.

She heard her mom hurrying down the stairs. "What's wrong?"

Abbie laughed. "Nothing. I didn't mean to scare you. Sorry. It's just that it's snowed overnight."

"It has? Let me see?" Her mom came and stood beside her and peered out into the yard. "It's so pretty, I love the snow."

"I know. You're like a little kid with it. Do you want to get bundled up, and we can go and walk around in it before it melts?"

Her mum grinned and hugged her. "Aww, I love that you'd do that with me. I know you're not so keen on it."

Abbie hugged her back tight. "I'm no snow bunny, but I'd do anything for you, Mom."

Her mom kissed her cheek. "Thanks, Abbs. Then you'll let me get my coffee and enjoy that before we go out there."

Abbie chuckled. "Of course. Coffee before all else. And unless you want to go for a walk, we don't even need to get dressed. We can just put our coats over our jammies and play in the back yard. Do you want to build a snowman?"

Her mom grinned. "You bet your ass I do. This is the best snow we've had down here in years. Your dad and I had started to go up into the mountains every year." She stopped, and her smile faded. "He'd love this."

Abbie squeezed her hand. "I know."

"Coffee."

Abbie knew to leave her alone with her coffee and her thoughts. If she was still feeling sad in a little while, they'd talk about Dad. But her mom tended to drift off in her mind to deal with her thoughts and then come back to reality, acting more composed. Abbie never really knew if she felt any better or if she just coped by putting on a brave face.

It seemed, however, that she didn't want to get lost in her thoughts. Instead, she asked, "How was last night? You were home early."

"Yeah. Neil is a very nice guy, but ..."

Her mom laughed. "Oh, my gosh, Abbs. He is so not your type."

She gave her mom a rueful smile. "Go on. You can say I told you so."

"I don't take any joy in that. I just want to see you happy. Even before I met him, I knew you didn't feel anything for him."

"I was hardly likely to feel anything for him. That was our first date."

"I don't mean real feelings that grow over time—I mean, you didn't feel any excitement, any spark. There was no way he was ever going to give you butterflies. I knew by the way you talked about him."

Abbie nodded. "I know. But he did help me to understand what you've been telling me about needing to be myself and to find someone who fits with who I really am."

Her mom grinned. "Well, then I like him. But I still don't like him as much as someone else I know. Someone who I'd guess does fit with who you really are."

Abbie raised an eyebrow and took a sip of her coffee in an attempt to hide her smile. "And who might that be?"

"You know exactly who I mean. Ivan! He gives you butterflies, doesn't he?"

Abbie nodded. "He does. I was being dumb, Mom. I thought I shouldn't go out with him."

"Why, though?"

"Because he's too much like me. He's taken some wrong turns in life. He likes to have fun. He's a free spirit." She sighed. "He's not looking to get married and produce offspring."

Her mom laughed. "I don't know why you kids think that's the way it works. You don't just decide that you're ready or you're not ready to settle down. You don't get to choose. The person who's meant for you just shows up in your life, and you fall for them, and being with them changes you and makes you want to get married because you can't imagine living your life without them. And then kids come along, or they don't. You don't make those decisions in a vacuum in advance. They grow out of what you do each day—who you meet, who you choose to go out with."

Abbie nodded. "I guess you're right. I hadn't thought about it that way. I kind of felt as though just going with the flow and letting life happen was how I got so screwed up—and drifted so far away from you and Dad. I thought that it was time to take control and do things right from now on."

Her mom reached across and squeezed her hand. "Try as you might, you can't control life—and especially not love. It comes when it's ready, whether that suits you or not." Her eyes filled with tears. "And it leaves before you're ready, too."

"It still lives in your heart, though, Mom. Just because he's not here doesn't mean he doesn't still love you."

Her mom sniffed and nodded. "It doesn't mean that I don't still love him either. Anyway. Tell me about Ivan before I start crying in my coffee."

"He's going to give me a call this morning. He remembered that you asked about him helping with a Christmas tree."

Her mom smiled. "You can say thank you anytime you like. I could tell the two of you had a thing for each other and that you were doing your best to mess it up. I planned to leave as many doors open for him as I could."

Abbie chuckled. "Thank you."

"Are the two of you going to do something together today, then?"

"I hope so. He said he'd call about the tree."

Her mom smiled. "Forget about that. You two should go off somewhere. Do something together."

"I'm not going to forget about it. I'm glad that you want to put one up."

Her mom sighed. "I do, and we will. But I might need a little more time to get used to the idea first."

"Okay." Her mom hadn't wanted to decorate for Christmas at all last year—they hadn't even really done Christmas. It hadn't felt right. Abbie was glad that she felt better about it this year, but she wanted to let her take things in her own time. "We'll forget about it for today. Do you want me to ask again tomorrow—or should I wait until you tell me?"

"I'll tell you. I do want one. It's just …" She gave Abbie a sad smile. "I need to come to terms with it first."

Abbie went to give her a hug, but she held up her coffee cup. "Why don't you go and dig out our snow boots while I finish this?"

~ ~ ~

Ivan pulled up outside Abbie's house a little before noon. When he'd called her earlier, she'd told him that they didn't need to get a tree today. At first, it'd seemed like she was having second thoughts about seeing him, but she'd assured him that wasn't the case. She did want to see him, it was just the Christmas tree shopping that was off.

He raised his hand to knock on the front door, but it opened before he could. Her mom stood there, grinning at him.

"Ivan! It's lovely to see you. Come on in."

"Thanks, Mrs. ..."

She gave him a stern look.

"Nina."

He followed her into the living room, where she offered him a seat. He sat down on the sofa, hoping that this didn't mean he was going to be here a while.

"Abbie will be down in a minute." Nina grinned. "We had a busy morning already, she needs to get changed." She looked over her shoulder before saying in a lower voice. "I'm glad you're here." She winked at him. "I was worried last night."

Ivan smiled. He wasn't sure how much she knew, but it didn't really matter. The important thing was that she was on his side. "Thanks. So was I."

"I'm surprised you didn't put up a fight."

"How could I?"

She laughed. "I know he was a bit weedy. You could have knocked him over with one finger."

Ivan chuckled. "I didn't mean that. And for what it's worth, he is a nice guy. I meant I have to respect her wishes."

"Aww. I knew there was a reason I liked you. As a guy, you're right; you do have to respect a girl's wishes. But as her mom, it was frustrating to see her wishing for the wrong thing. Especially for the wrong reasons."

Ivan nodded.

"I'm sorry. I don't want to embarrass you. I'm just glad you're here now. And I hope the two of you work something out."

"So do I."

Abbie came hurrying down the stairs. "Mom, do you want— oh! Hi! I didn't hear the door."

Her mom chuckled. "I let him in quietly because I wanted a word."

Abbie raised her eyebrows. "Should I be worried?"

"No. You're fine."

Abbie looked at Ivan. "Did she interrogate you or put you off somehow?"

He laughed. "Nope. We were just making friends."

"Hmm, I'm not sure if that's better or worse."

"It's better, Abbs," said her mom. "Much better. You need your people to like each other and be friends."

Ivan wondered what Abbie thought about her calling him one of her people. He liked the sound of it, but he wasn't sure that she would be so keen.

To his relief, she smiled. "I do need that, and it's such a refreshing change from last night. She wasn't as nice to Neil."

Ivan clenched his fists by his side. Neil was out of the picture now, but it still made his heart beat faster to think that he'd been here last night to take Abbie out.

Her mom caught his eye. He'd guess that she knew exactly what he was thinking—even if Abbie seemed oblivious.

"I wasn't mean to him."

"You weren't exactly friendly, either."

Her mom shrugged. "I don't think I would have liked him," she told Ivan.

"He's a good guy." He couldn't help but stand up for Neil.

"Oh, I'm sure he is. But …" She looked at Abbie. "Well, you know. Anyway. What are you two going to do with yourselves today?"

Abbie looked at him. "I don't know. I'm sure we'll think of something."

"You could go up to Stanton Falls. They're having that big Christmas market today."

It would make for a long day; they wouldn't get back until well after dark if they went now. But if Abbie was interested, Ivan was game to take her.

"That's your idea of fun, Mom."

"I don't mind taking you both if you want to go," Ivan volunteered before he stopped to think about it. A Christmas fair was something that only happened once a year. He'd hate to think her mom was missing out on it because of him.

They both stared at him.

"That's so sweet of you," said her mom. "But honestly, I couldn't face it yet. Maybe we can all go next year."

Ivan sucked in a deep breath. Next year? Was she seeing this as a long-term thing—even if Abbie wasn't?

Abbie had a weird look on her face—maybe she was freaked out by the thought of still seeing him this time next year. "Maybe we don't need to think about next year yet. It's too late to drive all the way up there today." She looked at Ivan. "I was thinking we could go over to the plaza at Four Mile Creek. We could poke around the stores and have some lunch over there?"

"That sounds great." He wasn't one for poking around stores, usually, but it was too cold to do much of anything outside.

"Drive carefully, won't you?" said her mom. "The roads might still be slippery."

"They're mostly clear now," said Ivan, "but I will drive carefully."

She smiled at him. "I know she's safe with you."

He wondered if she meant that as a chauffeur, he knew how to drive in any road conditions. From the way she was looking at him, he'd guess that she meant something more than that. It gave him a warm feeling in his chest—until he remembered that she wasn't the one he needed to convince—and Abbie didn't see him as someone who she'd want to look after her.

# Chapter Ten

Abbie stared out the window at the lake on the drive over to Four Mile. It looked so beautiful with snow on the shore and a now bright blue sky above.

"Are you okay over there?"

She turned to look at Ivan, and her breath caught in her chest. He was so damned gorgeous. "I'm good. Just admiring the view."

He shot a glance at her. "The lake—or me?"

She laughed. "Both. I have to say, you wear that jacket a lot better than Neil does."

He frowned.

Why in hell had she brought that up? It was because it was true. She'd been thinking that he looked so sexy in it—which reminded her that Neil hadn't. But she hadn't intended to bring up her stupid attempt to date someone else.

"The jacket? We didn't get him a jacket. Just jeans and a pullover."

"He said he went back to get one just like yours. Because you're so cool."

Ivan shook his head. "I didn't know about that. He's a nice guy. I just wish he could find a way to be comfortable in his own skin."

"Yeah. I think he figured out last night that that's what he needs to do."

"Did he really tell you you're not his type?"

She laughed. "He did. Apparently, he has a thing for a girl who works at the library."

"Sounds like she might be someone he'd have more in common with."

"Yeah."

"So why did he ask you out and not her?"

"I think because it'd matter to him if she said no. With me, I think he expected me to say no—and it didn't really matter if I did."

"He must be crazy."

She turned to look at him. "Why?"

"Because any guy in his right mind would want you to say yes."

She smiled. "You don't need to sweet-talk me. You got me."

He shot a glance at her. "I do?"

"Yeah." She reached over and took hold of his hand. "I'm yours to do as you want with."

He tightened his fingers around hers. "For how long?"

Wow. She hadn't expected he'd be too worried about that. "For as long as you like." She might as well be honest about it. He'd told her he wasn't interested in anything serious, but she'd be happy to see him until he got bored. She'd be sad when he did, but she knew how it went. She wanted him to know that she didn't have any expectations. She was willing to go with the flow.

He let go of her hand. Whether that was to keep both of his on the wheel or because he was thinking much shorter term than she was, she didn't know.

When they got to the plaza at Four Mile, he parked in the lot behind the clock tower. He cut the engine and turned to her with a serious look on his face. "Did you mean what you said before?"

"About what?"

"About you being mine—for as long as I like?"

She smiled. "Yep—and I meant the *to do as you want with* part too."

He let his gaze travel over her, making her shiver in anticipation of what she knew that look meant. She might wish that he was interested in something more, but that was all he was offering, and she wasn't about to complain.

He lifted his gaze and looked into her eyes. "I don't just want to sleep with you if that's what you're thinking."

"Oh! You don't?"

"No. I want us to date—for real."

She smiled. He was more of a gentleman than she'd initially given him credit for. He wasn't denying that he wanted to sleep with her—that wasn't in question, and he'd already said that he wanted to be her friend. That was all he meant. She couldn't allow herself to get carried away and read anything more than that into it. "Good. I'd like that."

"Okay." He looked as though he was about to say something else, but he changed his mind. "What stores do you want to poke around in?"

She laughed. "I didn't think you'd be much of a shopper, but I want to get you something."

"What kind of something?"

She opened the door and got out. Once he'd locked the car and they set off toward the shops, she smiled at him. "Something for your house. Whatever you'd like. A picture or a lamp or something that makes it look like you live there. At the moment, it looks like it's been staged ready to be sold or rented out."

He laughed. "You noticed?"

"It's hard not to. I'm hoping that if I get you a little something, it'll start the ball rolling, and you'll get some motivation to decorate a bit and make it your own." Her heart sank. "Unless you don't plan to stay long enough to make it your home?"

He took hold of her hand as they walked. "I do. I plan to be here for the long-term."

She smiled up at him. It made her happy to hear that—though she'd be happier if he said he wanted to be with her for the long-term. No! She didn't need to start thinking like that. She might have figured her shit out and come to understand that she could just be herself and hope that she'd meet the right guy someday. That didn't mean that he was the right guy—or even that he'd want to be.

"Ivan!"

They both turned at the sound of his name being called. Ivan wished he'd ignored it instead of reacting automatically. Whoever was shouting to him would no doubt be curious what he was doing out here with Abbie—and holding hands with her.

It was Colt. He lifted a hand and came hurrying toward them. "Are you guys late, too?"

"Late? What for?"

"Lunch. Everyone's meeting at the café, isn't that where you're going?"

Ivan shook his head. "No. We're shopping."

"Oh. Do you want to come? Logan, Angel, and Maria are all working today. So, Roxy, Luke, and Zack are coming to have lunch with them and Austin's bringing a couple of the girls over. I thought you were coming. You should." He smiled at Abbie. "You'll come, right?"

She looked at Ivan. He wasn't sure if she wanted to go or not, but she seemed to be deferring to him. Maybe she wanted to go but didn't want to drag him to join a crowd if he didn't want to.

"Come on in, guys. You're late. Everyone's here already." Roxy was standing on the terrace outside the café shouting to them.

Abbie made a face. "I guess that decides it."

To Ivan's disappointment, she let go of his hand as they followed Colt inside. Maybe she didn't want the others knowing they were together.

There was quite a crowd sitting around two tables. Everyone said hi, but he got the feeling there was some kind of undercurrent that he didn't get. Roxy, especially, was giving Abbie some weird looks that he didn't understand.

Angel smiled at them. "Sorry I didn't invite you. This started out as Luke coming over to meet me for lunch, and then it kind of snowballed from there."

"Snowball is the right word for it, today, too," said Maria. "Can you believe how much it snowed?"

Roxy grinned. "I love it!"

"I could have done without it today," said Austin. "I had to show a house halfway to Stanton, the roads were iffy out there." He looked at Ivan. "So, are you two a thing now? Did I not get the memo again?"

Ivan hesitated, but only for a moment. He didn't want to speak for Abbie, but he didn't want to make things too awkward either. "We are for today," he said with a smile. He hoped that might stop the others from asking any more questions that he didn't know how to answer. Of course, it had the opposite effect.

Logan turned to Abbie. "You didn't waste any time." Roxy shot him a warning look, but it didn't do anything to shut him up. "What happened last night?"

Abbie scowled at him. "Nothing—not that it's any of your business."

"Were you okay?" asked Roxy. "I thought Kenzie was out of order, but I figured you didn't need an audience."

Ivan wondered just what exactly had happened.

"Kenzie was just being Kenzie. She helped me out, really." To Ivan's surprise, she turned and smiled up at him. "She helped me realize that I was making a mistake."

Logan laughed. "Any one of us could have told you that. You and Neil?" He laughed again.

Zack shot a worried look at Ivan, but he smiled. He imagined this must all sound confusing to someone who didn't know what was going on. Luckily, he did.

Abbie scowled at Logan. "If anyone's going to criticize me for being out with Neil last night and then being here with Ivan today, I don't think it should be you, Perkins."

Ivan tensed, hoping this wasn't going to get ugly.

He needn't have worried. Logan grinned. "You won't catch me casting any stones in your direction, girl. I was just shocked when I saw you with him last night." He smiled at Ivan. "I'm much happier to see you with this guy today."

He sensed Abbie relax by his side. "Okay. Sorry. I didn't mean to bite your head off. I think it's probably me who thinks I must be a shitty human being."

"If you do, you're the only one," said Maria. "We've all had bad dates—and I don't think any one of us would have turned down a good one the next day."

"I know I wouldn't," Roxy agreed.

Logan slung his arm around her shoulders. "No more dates for you, babe. You're nearly a married woman."

Ivan smiled at the way she nodded happily. "I'm not the only one either."

The girls started chatting about weddings, and Ivan realized that there would be three of them at some point in the near future. He cast a sideways glance at Abbie. No. He couldn't start thinking like that. Even if he wanted to, it'd be pointless. She didn't see him that way.

~ ~ ~

It was late afternoon by the time they got back to town. Other than the initial awkwardness at lunch, Abbie had had a great time. Ivan was good company. It felt like they'd known each other forever. He was easy-going, and she knew he understood where she was coming from. He was like Kenzie in that way. Part of her wanted to know what his story was— what he'd lived through that made him so non-judgmental. Another part of her knew better than to ask.

"Do you want me to drop you off at home?"

She looked at him as he turned onto Main Street. "Is that what you want?"

He smiled. "I think you know it isn't, but I don't know if you need to get back to your mom. Or if you've had enough of me."

She leaned across and rested her hand on his thigh, hoping that might give him an idea of what she wanted. "I'll call Mom and make sure she's doing okay, but I don't need to go home yet."

"Okay. Do you want to come to my place? You can help me hang that picture, and if you like, we can order something for dinner."

"That sounds good to me." She pulled her phone out of her purse. "I'll just check in with Mom."

"Hey, Abbs."

"Hi, Mom. How are you doing?"

"I'm great, thanks. I made a casserole for dinner. I didn't think you'd be coming back to eat, but I wanted to make something just in case."

"I can come and have dinner with you if you like?"

"No! You do your thing. Have dinner with Ivan. I wasn't hinting that I wanted you home, I was just letting you know that there's something here for you."

Abbie smiled. Her mom tried in so many different little ways to let her know that she thought about her—that she loved her. "Thanks, Mom. You're the best."

"It's the least I can do. Look at everything you've done for me this last year. I don't think I'd ever have gotten back on my feet if you hadn't come home and helped me through it."

"Hey. I needed you as much as you needed me."

"In some ways, maybe. But I didn't mean to get all mushy on you. Are you still with Ivan?"

"Yes. If you're okay, I'm going to have dinner at his place."

Her mom was quiet for a long moment.

"Is that okay?"

"Of course, it is! I'm just trying to figure out the best way to say that I don't expect you back tonight."

Abbie pursed her lips. "I'll be home." As much as she'd love to spend the night with Ivan, she didn't want her mom thinking that she was going back to her old ways.

"I'm not going to argue with you, Abbs. I'm just saying."

"I know."

"Just text me and let me know either way. I'll worry if I don't hear."

"Okay. I will. What are you going to do?"

"Never mind me. Go on. Go and have fun with Ivan. I love you."

"Love you, too, Mom. See you later."

By the time she hung up, Ivan was pulling through the gates into his driveway. He drove straight into the garage and smiled at her when he stopped. "Is she okay?"

"Yeah. She's fine."

"And you told her that you'll be home tonight?"

Abbie nodded. She wished she hadn't, but it was the right thing to do. "Do you mind?"

"Mind?!"

"You know what I mean. We both know what's going to happen here. Were you expecting me to stay?"

"Abbie, Abbie, Abbie." He reached out and touched her cheek. "You need to understand—I don't have any expectations here. I'm just happy to take what I can get."

"Okay." She kind of wished that he'd said yes; that he'd been hoping she would spend the night with him. She wanted to. But she had to remember where he was coming from. He wasn't looking to build to anything, just to have some fun and some sex.

He tucked his fingers under her chin and lifted it, so she had to look him in the eye. "I know you want to be there for your mom. I get it."

Aww. Every time she thought he didn't care, he showed her just how caring and understanding he was.

He carried the picture that she'd bought for him into the house and set it down on the island in the kitchen. "Where do you think it should go?"

"I thought it'd look good in the living room, above the sofa."

He carried it through and held it against the wall. "You're right. It does. I don't suppose I could hire you to be my interior designer, could I?"

She laughed. "Err. No. I don't know what I'm doing. I just know that a splash of color has to help. You just need to start buying things when you see them. It's not about design as such, just about making your mark on the place."

"I know. I've never done that before."

"Well, this is an awesome place to start. I love this house."

"Yeah. I know I'm lucky. It comes with the job, though. It's not mine."

"I know." Part of her wanted to be mad at him. Was he warning her off again—thinking that she was some gold-digger who might set her sights on him just because he lived in a nice house?

She went to stand in front of the windows and looked out at the lake. "This view is so beautiful."

He came and stood behind her and slid his arms around her waist. "It's not as beautiful as you are."

She wanted to tell him that he didn't need to feed her any lines. But she'd already made that clear. And ... she closed her eyes as he nuzzled his lips into her neck. It felt good; the way her body responded to his warm breath on her skin and the way her chest filled with warmth when he told her she was beautiful. She wanted to believe he was saying it just because he meant it.

She leaned back against him. "You're pretty hot yourself, mister."

He put his hands on her hips and pulled her back against him. He was hard, his cock pressed into her ass, and she moved it against him.

Instead of pushing her skirt up, like she'd expected him to, he turned her around to face him. She slid her arms up around his neck, he looked down into her eyes.

"I want you, Abbie."

"I want you, too. Do you want to take it upstairs?"

His eyebrows knit together, and he shook his head, making her wonder what was wrong with that suggestion. "I didn't mean—"

"Oh!" She felt stupid. "You didn't mean yet?"

He tightened his arms around her waist and pulled her against him. "I meant ..." He almost looked as though he was in pain. "I didn't mean ..." He shook his head. "Never mind."

She ran her fingers down his cheek, not knowing what his problem was, but having a pretty good idea of how she might fix it. "Kiss me. Then tell me what you want."

He started to say something, but she sank her fingers in his hair and pulled his head down to her. "We can talk about it later." She nipped at his bottom lip.

That seemed to end all his hesitation. He claimed her mouth in a kiss that left her leaning against him for support. His tongue slid inside her mouth, mating with hers. He stole her senses. It felt as though he was kissing the world away, the past, the future—they ceased to exist. There was only the two of them, locked in each other's arms, kissing as if it were the only thing keeping them alive.

# Chapter Eleven

Ivan set his plate down on the coffee table. They'd ordered pizza from Giuseppe's; that was the second night in a row for him, but that was what she'd wanted.

Abbie was still munching a slice. He swallowed as he watched her lick her finger. He didn't know if she was doing that for his benefit. He had a feeling she might be. She'd made it plain that she'd wanted him to take her to bed when they first got here. But fool that he was, he'd sidestepped it. The way she'd kissed him had almost persuaded him, but he wanted to hang out with her—not just sleep with her. There'd be time for that—he hoped. She wasn't going to stay the night, but it was still early.

Last time she'd been here, he'd given in to his desire for her, but he'd regretted it since. Maybe regret was too strong a word. What had happened in the kitchen wasn't something he'd ever consider regrettable. But things were different now. Tonight was the beginning of something. Maybe not the beginning of something serious, even if he wished that it might be.

She smiled at him. "What are you thinking?"

He shrugged. "I'm thinking that I had a good time today."

"Me, too."

"And I'm hoping that we'll have lots more days like this."

She set her plate on the coffee table beside his and moved closer to him on the sofa. "You are? I'd like that."

He put his arm around her shoulders and looked down into her eyes. A picture of Logan and Roxy this afternoon flashed into his mind. Logan had looked so happy and confident when he'd told Roxy that there'd be no more dates for her—that she was his and they'd be married soon. He wondered how that must feel. To his surprise, he wanted to find out.

"I know I'm not what you're looking for. But I think we can have a lot of fun together."

Her eyes lit up, and she smiled. "I think so, too."

He hugged her closer, hoping that maybe, over time, she might start to see him differently.

Her next words dashed that hope. She rested her hand on his thigh. "I'm looking forward to some fun later."

He closed his eyes. His body was agreeing with her. It wanted the same kind of fun she did. But his mind wished that she'd understand he wanted a different kind of fun, too. He wanted them to have the same kind of fun Logan and Roxy did, teasing each other, laughing at shared jokes. Making plans for their future.

"Too soon?" she asked. "Sorry. I'll clean up."

He frowned as he watched her get to her feet.

She gave him a rueful smile. "What can I say? I'm horny for you. But straight after dinner isn't ideal, is it?"

He shook his head. He didn't care about having just eaten, but he couldn't tell her what he'd really been thinking.

He followed her through to the kitchen and she rinsed the dishes and he put them in the dishwasher. He couldn't help but think that this could be their life if she lived with him, if they were together.

She dried her hands and smiled at him. "I feel so comfortable with you."

He wanted to tell her that he felt comfortable with her too. But he meant that he felt comfortable having her in his space, doing dishes with her. She only meant that she was relaxed enough with him that she didn't mind being open about wanting to get him into bed.

They went and sat back down on the sofa, and she snuggled into his side. "Talk to me."

He gave her a half smile. "What about?" He half expected that she wanted him to talk dirty to her, and he was ready to. He needed to get out of his head, and the best way he could think of to do that would be to get into her pants.

He had it wrong again, though.

"Tell me about who you are? About your family. About your life."

Each time he thought he had her figured out, she shifted the goalposts on him. "Why do you want to know?"

Her smile faded. "I want to get to know you better. I told you that. Or is that too much? Do you want to just keep this casual? I don't want to be that chick who only wants to talk when you want to …"

This was frustrating as hell! He couldn't do it. He couldn't keep guessing or keep her guessing. He turned to her and cupped her face between his hands.

She raised an eyebrow at him. "Does this mean you just want to …?"

"No, Abbie, it doesn't." He dropped a kiss on her lips. "It means I want to tell you something, and I want to look you in the eye and watch your reaction when I do."

She waggled her eyebrows. "Are you going to tell me what you're into and ask if I want to?"

He smiled through pursed lips. "Yes."

Her eyes widened a little. He didn't know what she was expecting him to say, but he knew she wasn't expecting this.

"Will you promise me that you won't be mad at me, won't tell me that I'm crazy—and that you won't storm out in disgust?"

"Err. I think so. But I can't make any promises. I mean, if you're into some serious kink, then I can tell you now that I'm not your girl."

He smiled. He couldn't drag it out any longer. "Okay. What I'm into is you."

Her eyebrows knit together. "I thought we'd already established that."

"On some level, yeah—but not on the level that I need you to understand. You keep talking like I only want to be your fuck-buddy."

She nodded.

"I want more than that. I know you don't see me as someone you'd want more with, but I need you to know that I see you that way. If all you want from me is sex, I'm not going to say no. But I'm driving myself crazy here. Watching what I say, trying not to scare you off. I'd rather get it out in the open than walk on eggshells the whole time. I like you, Abbie. I'd like you to be my girlfriend, and I don't know how that sounds—and I don't know if you'll walk out the door now."

She stared back into his eyes. As the moments dragged on before she spoke, he was convinced that he'd blown it. She'd told him from the beginning that he wasn't the right kind of guy for her. He wasn't going to take it back, though—wasn't going to apologize. It was better to be upfront.

"Wow!" she said eventually.

He shrugged and gave her a rueful smile. "I have to be honest, even if it's not what you want to hear."

She shook her head rapidly. "No! I didn't mean it like that." She smiled and planted a kiss on his lips. "You don't get it. That's exactly what I've wanted to hear from you, but I didn't think ..." She frowned. "You told me that first night we went for a drink that you weren't ... You weren't ... interested in anything serious with me."

He frowned. "I didn't say that! You said that I wasn't what you were looking for and when you told me that you needed someone ..." He stopped to remember what exactly she had said. "Oh. You said we were too much alike." He frowned as he tried to recall the conversation. She'd said she needed to get married and settle down and have two-point-four kids.

He looked into her eyes. "I said I wasn't going to marry you and produce offspring."

She nodded. Her cheeks were flushed, and she looked uncomfortable.

"I was only repeating what you'd said."

"I didn't know what the hell I was talking about. I still thought that I needed to set up some perfect little life and conform to what I thought was expected of a nice girl."

He had to laugh. "You are a nice girl."

She made a face. "You know what I mean."

He nodded. He did.

She blew out a sigh. "Okay. You've been honest with me. I owe you the same. Do you want to know what I've been thinking all evening—all day?"

"That you wish I'd hurry up and screw you so you can go home?"

She scowled. "No! That I wish I hadn't screwed things up between us that night we went for a drink. That I wish we hadn't gone out until after I figured out how stupid I was being, thinking I needed to squish myself into a life that wouldn't suit me."

She reached up and touched his cheek. "Also, that I wish you hadn't been so straightforward when you told me that you wouldn't want anything serious with me."

He smiled. "Are you saying what I think you are?"

"I'm saying that yes, I'd love to be your girlfriend." She smiled back at him. "I still want to screw your brains out, but I think it'll be even better now."

"Now that you know that I want more than your body?"

She chuckled. "Now that you know that I want more than yours."

He wrapped his arm around her and drew her closer. He loved the feel of her full, soft breasts against his chest. "You want more than my body?" He tangled his fingers in her hair and kissed her deeply before lifting his head.

She nodded breathlessly. "I do, but I want more of your body first."

He leaned forward until she lay back on the sofa. "I want more of your body, too."

She wrapped her arms around his neck and pulled him down to her. He loved that she wasn't shy about what she wanted. Her hands roved over him as they kissed. She spread her legs and rubbed herself against him, making him ache to be inside her.

His head was still reeling from the revelations that she was as eager to explore this as he was. His body was more interested in exploring hers. He moaned as her fingers found his zipper and then found their way inside his boxers.

"I want more of this," she murmured.

He cupped her breast with one hand and closed the other around her ass. "You're about to get it."

~ ~ ~

They were naked in a matter of seconds. Abbie had been hoping that they'd make it to his bed this time. But that hardly mattered. What mattered was this was about more than sex now.

She closed her eyes as he dipped his head and sucked her nipple. She sank her fingers in his hair and moaned her pleasure. He grazed her with his teeth, sending warning signals racing through her body. She reached down, wanting to touch him, to prime him, but he moved his hips away.

"Let me taste you," he breathed.

She relaxed back on the sofa. If he wanted to make it about her, she wasn't going to refuse. She closed her eyes while he cupped her breasts between his hands and tormented her with his lips and tongue. She arched her back as he worked his way down over her rib cage. She knew what came next, and she spread her legs in eager anticipation.

Her fingers tangled in his hair as he trailed his tongue over her. He was good. He knew what he was doing and … oh! She had to let go of his hair, or she might pull it out, that felt so … She clutched at the cushions underneath her. He was kissing her, kissing her deeply, and her lips were opening up to him so he could slide his tongue inside and … oh!

"Ivan!" she gasped.

Without breaking his rhythm, he cupped his hands under her ass, lifting her up to give him better access. His tongue slid deeper, and her stomach tightened. He was going to make her …

Her orgasm took her, and she let herself go. It felt as though his talented tongue was carrying her away on a tide of pleasure. She was totally at his mercy, and she loved every second of it.

When she stilled, he lifted his head and smiled.

"Oh my God!" she breathed.

He chuckled. "Not quite a god, but I'm not bad."

She pushed herself up on her elbows. "And confident in your abilities, too, huh?"

He shrugged. "Why not be?"

"I like it. I'm pretty confident I can return the favor." She knew she could make him feel as good as he'd just made her feel. She reached for him, but he shook his head with a playful smile.

"But I want to." She knew guys loved that. She did, too. She wanted to taste him.

He slid his hand between her legs, and she shuddered as his fingers teased her. "I'd love that. But right now, I want to be inside you."

Something about the way he said it melted her insides. She needed him to tell her.

"What do you want to do?"

He raised an eyebrow, and she nodded, hoping he'd understand.

He did. "I want to lie back and watch you ride me."

She got to her knees as he lay back against the cushions.

He closed his hands around her hips and positioned her above him. He guided himself toward her with his hand, and she rubbed herself against him. He was so hot and hard; she was aching to feel him inside her. He didn't seem to be in a hurry. He was caressing her clit with his tip, watching her face as he did.

"Does that feel good?"

She nodded and cupped her breasts in her hands. "I'm going to need you to fuck me."

His eyes glazed with lust as he watched her tease her nipples into tight little peaks. "Give it to me," he breathed.

She shook her head and continued touching herself. "Take it."

His hands tightened around her hips, and he pulled her down hard, making her gasp as his thick hard shaft filled her.

They moved together in a frantic rhythm as he drove deeper and deeper. His gaze didn't leave her breasts as they bounced above him. She wasn't going to last. She was already on the edge, but he slowed, leaving her wriggling, desperately needing him to finish her. Instead, he pulled her down to him and kissed her. One hand closed around the back of her head, the other grasped her ass. He moved so slowly it was exquisite torment. She tightened around him as he inched deeper inside her then just when she was about to go over the edge, he pulled back just as slowly, leaving her panting desperately for him to finish her.

The tension built and built in her belly as his cock and his tongue slid deep inside her, took her almost to the edge and then withdrew. She wanted to get back to the pounding rhythm they'd set at first, but he held her tight and moved her in his time.

The pleasure was mounting relentlessly between her legs. She wanted to hurtle her way toward release, but he took her there so damned slowly, she felt like she might implode. She writhed against him, needing him to … and he did. He thrust his hips hard, making her scream. Now. His thrusts were frantic, burying himself deeper and deeper inside her until she felt him tense and grow harder still.

"Abbie!" he gasped.

His release triggered her own, and they carried each other away to a place where nothing existed except the two of them. Where nothing mattered except the feel of him inside her, the feel of his hands on her and their frenzied movements as they soared on waves of pleasure.

She finally slumped down on him, and he closed his arms around her.

"So, you're going to be my girlfriend, right?"

She lifted her head and looked down into his eyes. She was more used to guys who wanted to wriggle out of promises after sex—not ones who wanted to hold her to them. She nodded, wondering what he was going to say next.

He smiled and ran his fingers through her hair. "Good, because we need to do this every day, at least once a day."

She chuckled. "That can be arranged."

His eyes were a deeper blue as he looked into hers. "I like the sound of that."

# Chapter Twelve

Ivan slowed the treadmill to a walk. He'd gotten a good workout in this morning. He smiled. Not as good as he'd gotten with Abbie last night. She was insatiable! After the sofa, they'd taken it upstairs to his bed. He shifted in his shorts at the memory of how she'd repaid him, as she called it, for the way he'd tasted her. Then, before she left, he'd taken her in the shower, hard, against the wall with the water running down over her full breasts. He blew out a sigh. His cock was coming to life at the memory.

He looked around, feeling as though someone might see him and read his thoughts. There was no one here. There'd been a couple of guys when he first came in, but now the place was empty.

He got down from the treadmill and got a drink of water. He'd taken Abbie home just after eleven. He got that she wanted to be there for her mom, but he hoped that with time, she'd want to stay with him, too. He was thrilled at the way she'd reacted to his confession that he wanted to explore a real relationship with her. But he didn't see how that could happen if she didn't ever want to stay with him. It was a big thing in his mind. If you were just screwing around, then you went home afterward. If you were a real a couple, then you slept together—in the more literal sense, as well.

He went over to the weight bench and set his water bottle down. He hadn't lifted since the beginning of the week. He needed to put some time in. It was a good way to spend the morning. He'd thought he might spend the day with Abbie but she'd called to say she had plans with her mom. She was going to call him later. He hoped that meant he'd get to see her this afternoon or evening. He'd asked about getting the Christmas tree, but she'd told him that her mom was struggling with that. She wanted to decorate, but it was hard for her since Abbie's dad had passed. He wondered if there might be anything he could do to help—to ease things for her. But it was probably best if he left that alone. Grief was a very individual process, and it wasn't his place to interfere in it.

"Hey, big guy."

He snapped back to the present moment when Logan came toward him from the locker room.

"I thought I'd have the place to myself. What are you doing here? I thought you'd be sleeping in with Abbie this morning."

Ivan frowned. He didn't like the assumption that Abbie would have stayed with him last night. "No."

"Sorry. Did I hit a nerve? Did that not work out?"

"It worked out okay."

Logan gave him a raunchy grin. "She's quite a girl. I'm glad you figured things out with her."

"Me, too."

"Are you two an item now, then?"

"Yeah."

"Casual … or …?"

Ivan frowned at him. "More than casual, why?"

"Just curious. She used to be a real party girl, but since she came back to the lake, she's been more like a nun."

Ivan nodded.

"I guess I'm curious if you two are going to take each other back to old ways or if you're going to be good for each other."

"Why do you think it's any of your business?"

Logan held up a hand. "It isn't. You're right. Sorry. It's no excuse, but in my defense, I'm only saying it because I think the two of you might be good for each other."

"Thanks. Sorry I bit your head off. I forget that's the way it works around here, everyone knows everyone's business and thinks they get a say in it."

Logan laughed. "I should know better than to stick my nose in. I've told the girls often enough that they shouldn't interfere; now, I'm doing the same thing."

"It's okay. I know you mean well."

"So, are you two seeing each other with an eye on something more—or screwing each other with your minds on nothing else?"

Ivan had to laugh. "It's still none of your business, but since I know that until not so long ago, you were the kind who was only into screwing, so you're not judging, I'll tell you. I'm hoping for something more."

"Does she know that?"

"Yep, she says that's what she wants, too."

Logan grinned. "I was hoping that was it. You'll be part of the couples crowd soon."

"I hope so."

"I'll keep 'em crossed for you."

"Thanks."

"One more question?"

"What?"

"Do you plan to stay here for good?"

Ivan shrugged. "It's where my job is."

"I know, but before you go all in, you should probably be sure you want to stay here. Abbie's never going to leave. She's sworn up and down that she'll never move away from her mom again."

Ivan nodded. He knew that. Of course, he did. It just hadn't occurred to him what it really meant. He was happy here in Summer Lake. He was enjoying small-town life. But would he enjoy it so much if he knew that this was it for him? If things got really serious between Abbie and him, would he be happy to spend the rest of his days here—or at least, the rest of her mom's days?

Logan smiled at him. "And now I've given you something to chew on, I'd better get doing. See you around. I'll give you a call next time everyone's getting together. Invite the two of you along."

"Thanks." Ivan sat down on the weight bench. He didn't think he'd have a problem staying here, but Logan was right— he should probably be sure about it before he and Abbie went all in.

~ ~ ~

"You've been very quiet this morning. Did things go well yesterday?"

Abbie nodded happily. "They did, Mom. They went even better than I thought they might."

"So, am I going to be seeing more of Ivan—and less of you—around here?"

That wiped the smile off her face. "I hope you'll be seeing more of Ivan, but you won't be seeing any less of me. I'm here for you, Mom."

Her mom waved a hand. "Don't be silly, love. Of course, that's the way it'll go. When you meet someone, you spend a lot of time with them. You could have stayed there last night, you know. You didn't need to come back here."

Abbie wanted to tell her that she shouldn't have stayed with a guy on their first real date, regardless of whether she needed to get home to her mom or not. But that would be just too hypocritical. She and Ivan hadn't needed the whole night to have all the sex they wanted. "Maybe I'll stay over at his place at some point. But this is just the beginning for us, Mom. I don't know if it'll even work out."

"I do. I really think he's the one for you, Abbie. And I couldn't be happier."

Abbie sighed.

"What's wrong?"

"Honestly? I hope he's the one. But I don't want to rush this. You have to remember that only a couple of days ago, I was telling myself that he couldn't be the one because he wasn't suitable."

"No, you need to forget that. You've come to your senses— I'm very glad to see. And now that you have, you need to get on with it. He's lovely. He likes you a lot. You like him a lot. All I'm saying is that I'm glad you've figured out that you need to follow your heart instead of all that doing what you think is the right thing. I hope you won't take much longer to come to your senses about the rest of it, too."

"The rest of what?"

"Come on, Abbs. You don't need to stay here with me forever—you don't have to stay another minute if you don't want to. I'm grateful that you came back and for all that you've done. But you've done enough. I need to get back on my own feet, and you need to find yours."

Abbie stared at her.

She laughed. "I'm not saying I want you gone or anything, but I am asking you to stop using me as an excuse."

"An excuse?"

"Yes. It's time for you to figure out what you want in life and go after it—instead of saying that you can't because you have to put me first. I'm officially releasing you of any obligation to your poor old mom."

"It's not an obligation. I want to help you."

"And you have helped me. I couldn't have gotten through without you. But now, it's time for the next step."

Abbie blew out a sigh. "I don't want to let you down again."

"You won't. You never did. You made some mistakes, but that's called being human. We never thought any less of you.

You never let us down. I'm so proud of you, proud of the way you've turned your life around. But everything you've done has been for me, not for yourself. It's time to make Abbie happy now."

"Making Abbie happy was what took me to the city and messed my life up."

"That was the younger, wilder Abbie who didn't know any better. Now you do. Now you can make better choices. And that's enough. I'm not going to keep harping on about it. Just know that I love you. And what will make me happy is seeing you happy—truly happy."

"Thanks, Mom. I love you." Abbie leaned in to hug her.

"I love you, too."

"And thanks for coming with me this morning."

Abbie nodded. Sometimes her mom went to the cemetery by herself, but this morning, she'd asked Abbie to go with her. That was way more important to her than a tentative plan to go over to Ivan's. No matter what her mom might say, for things like that, she would always come first.

"Are you seeing Ivan today?"

"Maybe later. I said I'd call him around lunchtime."

Her mom smiled. "Well, if the two of you don't have any other plans, I'm ready for that Christmas tree whenever you want to pick one up."

"Okay. I'll ask if he wants to help get one."

"Only if you don't have other plans."

Abbie smiled. "We don't."

Ivan took hold of Abbie's hand as they wandered around the Christmas tree lot. It made him smile to watch her examine all of the trees. She was as eager as a little kid.

"What do you think of this one?"

He chuckled. "I'd have to say that to me, it looks just like all the others."

She gave him a disbelieving look. "You can't be serious? You're not telling me that you can't see the difference between that tall scraggly one over there and this one which is perfectly shaped?"

"That's exactly what I'm telling you. All I see is a bunch of trees. Granted, it's obvious that some of them are taller than the others, but other than that, I wouldn't have a clue."

She frowned at him. "Didn't you have a Christmas tree as a kid?"

"Yeah. At least, for a few years, we did. But it was a plastic one. You know, one of those that comes with the lights already part of it?"

"Aww. You poor thing. You didn't ever know the magic of a real Christmas tree?"

"Until now, I didn't know there was any magic to a real Christmas tree."

She laughed. "Well, now, you do. See this one?"

He nodded.

"This one is very special. Look at the shape; it's perfectly proportioned."

He let his gaze rove over her. "I can appreciate perfect proportions."

She pushed at his arm. "Focus! I'm serious. This is important. Your education in life has been seriously lacking to this point if you don't know about Christmas trees. I am trying to educate you. I'm trying to do you a favor."

He waggled his eyebrows at her. "If you want to do me a favor, you can give me a rundown on perfect proportions when we get back to my place."

She gave him a stern look. "How could I sleep with a guy who doesn't appreciate a good Christmas tree?"

He laughed. "I can think of a few ways, but since I'm getting the idea that you're actually serious about this, I'll save them for later. Go ahead, educate my sorry ass about the magic of Christmas trees."

"Okay, this one is about as perfect as it can get. Now I'll show you some that aren't. You need to know what won't work for you so that you can recognize what will when you find it."

She was talking about Christmas trees, but he saw the parallel with finding a partner. "That might be the way it works for you, but the way I see it, why would I bother looking at any more when I know I found the perfect one?"

"Because if you don't know any better, you might think the wrong one is perfect."

He closed his arms around her waist and dropped a kiss on her lips. "But I wasn't even looking, and the perfect one landed in my lap. I don't want to look at any more."

She searched his face, finally understanding what he was getting at. "But what about next year? You'll need to get another one next year."

He smiled. "That's not the way I work. Remember, I grew up with an artificial tree. Once you find one of those, you get to keep it forever."

"Can I help you?"

"Yes." Ivan smiled at the guy who was running the lot. "I'll show you the one I want."

He went back to the tree Abbie had described as perfect and pointed at it. "This is the one." He looked at Abbie to check, and she smiled.

"You have a good eye. This one is a beauty," said the guy.

Ivan winked at Abbie. "What can I say? I have good taste."

"I hope you don't mind paying for what you like. This one is a hundred bucks."

Ivan pulled his wallet out of his pocket.

Abbie shook her head rapidly and pulled out her purse.

"Please let me?" asked Ivan. "I'd like to do this for your mom."

She made a face. "You don't need to do that."

"I know, but I want to. I like that she asked me to help get one. I especially like that she's been on my side since the beginning. If you don't mind, I'd like to do this." A thought struck him. "But I won't push it if it's something special that you want to do for her."

"No, it's not that. I just don't want you to feel like you have to."

The guy smiled at them. "Let him buy you the tree, lady. If a guy can win brownie points with his mother-in-law over the holidays, you don't stand in the way of that."

Ivan half expected her to correct the guy, to tell him that they weren't married, but she just smiled and nodded. "Thank you."

The guy sent one of his assistants to help Ivan get the tree tied on top of his car. Once it was secured and the guy had gone, Abbie came to him and stood on her tiptoes to plant a kiss on his cheek.

"That was so sweet of you. Thank you."

"I need you to understand that I'm telling the truth when I say it really is my pleasure. I know Christmas will be rough for your mom." He frowned. "I'm sorry, sweetie, I guess it will be hard on you too. You're always so focused on how your mom feels, but you have your own feelings to deal with as well."

She shrugged. "If you want to know the truth, I just feel guilty. Of course, I'm sad. I miss him. It kills me that I hadn't seen him for a while before he died. But it's Mom's feelings that matter. I don't deserve —"

He put a finger to her lips and slipped his other arm around her waist and pulled her closer. "I'm not usually a bossy guy, but I will tell you I don't want to hear you say those three words again."

"Which three words?"

"You said you don't deserve."

"But you didn't even let me finish the sentence. You don't know what I was going to say."

"It doesn't matter what you were going to say. There's nothing you could say that would make that sentence true. I've told you before, and I'll tell you again, you deserve the world, Abbie."

She buried her face in his chest, and he hugged her close.

"It's true; I'm not just saying it. You need to believe it."

She looked up into his eyes. "That first night, when we went for a drink, you offered to be my friend and to help me chase the blues away when I was feeling down. At the time, I thought you just wanted an in, an open door for a one-nighter when I was feeling down. I couldn't have been more wrong about you, could I?"

He smiled. "Maybe, at the time, you weren't entirely wrong. But now, I need you to know that I want to be here for you, no matter what."

She looked into his eyes, and he could feel a change in her. If she didn't believe him, she wanted to. And maybe she relaxed just a little, accepting that he had her back.

# Chapter Thirteen

When they got back to the house, Abbie's mom greeted her with a smile. "Did you find one?"

Abbie nodded happily. "We did, and it's perfect, Mom. You're going to love it."

Her mom looked up the path to where Ivan was untying the tree from his car. "Oh, wow! It's a big one. Do you think we need to go and give him a hand with it?"

"He said he's fine." She chuckled. "I think it's a guy thing. You know? He needs to do it by himself and not need the help of a little lady."

Her mom chuckled with her. "Oh, I do know. I know all too well. Your dad was exactly the same. My job was to pick out the tree but getting it home and getting it set up that was all down to him."

Abbie could tell she was getting upset. Her eyes were shiny, and she clasped her hands together.

"Well, you might want to stay here in case he needs a hand, but even if he does, I'm sure he won't want both of us. I'll go inside and make us some hot chocolate."

Abbie wanted to go after her, but she knew better. She needed a moment to compose herself before Ivan came in.

She turned back to check on him. It didn't look like he was going to need any help at all. He already had the tree over his shoulder and was heading toward the gate. She rushed up the path to open it for him before he got there.

"Thanks. Is your mom okay?"

"She'll be fine. She's making some hot chocolate."

"Great. Where am I going with this thing? Do you want it in the living room?"

"Yes, please. You might just have to lean it in the corner for now. I didn't think. I should have set up the little table that we put it on."

"We can figure that out." He adjusted it on his shoulder. "The first thing is to get it in there."

Abbie was surprised to see that her mom had set the table up. She'd even gotten the skirt out and the decorations, too.

Ivan set the tree down and leaned it against the wall. "You have to remember that I've never dealt with one of these before. Do I just stick it in that bucket?"

She laughed. "That's the idea."

He had the tree set up, and she was arranging the skirt over the bucket and the table by the time her mom came into the living room. She looked like she'd recovered a little. Abbie could tell that she'd been crying, but she didn't imagine Ivan would notice.

"That's wonderful! Thank you so much. I hope you like hot chocolate. I know it's not much in the way of a thank you, but it's the first and most immediate thing I do."

Ivan smiled at her. "I love hot chocolate, thank you. I haven't had it since I was a kid."

"Aww." Abbie looked at him. "You're just a poor Christmas deprived soul, aren't you?"

He made a face at her. "I guess I might be, by your standards. But if it's any consolation, I never felt like I was missing out on anything."

"I should have warned you that Abbie is a bit of a Christmas nut," said her mom. "In fact, I'm surprised to see you both back so soon. I thought she'd have you out there all afternoon in search of the perfect one."

Her words reminded Abbie of the way Ivan had talked about finding the perfect one. She smiled at him. "I found it pretty much straight away. I just couldn't believe I was that lucky. I was going to look around to make sure, but Ivan was smart enough to show me that there was no need."

The smile on his face told her he understood what she was trying to tell him. Her mom looked as though she understood as well.

"That's great," she said. "I'll go and get us that hot chocolate. Would you like some cookies, too?" She raised an eyebrow at Ivan.

He nodded rapidly. "Yes, please."

"I'll be right back."

Once she'd gone, Abbie went to him and kissed his cheek. "Thank you."

"I told you, it's my pleasure."

"I don't mean about paying for the tree. I mean for helping me figure out that when I find the perfect one, I should try to keep him."

He looked surprised that she said it so openly, but he'd been open with her—and patient, too, now she came to think about it. How many guys would have been as cool as he was that she'd chosen to go on a date with someone else? And if he hadn't been so open with her last night—about wanting to see where things could go between them, she'd still be second-guessing everything he said—thinking that he wasn't interested in her as anything more than a booty call.

"You don't know if he's perfect yet."

She smiled. "I have a pretty good idea, and the rest will only come with time."

He smiled. "I'm far from perfect, Abbie. I hope when you discover the flaws that they're not too much for you to deal with."

"I doubt that." She stepped away from him when her mom came back into the room, carrying a tray.

"Here, let me get that." Ivan took it from her before Abbie could offer. He set it down on the coffee table.

Abbie's mom smiled at her. "Good-looking and a gentleman, too. I like him, Abbs."

Abbie laughed, hoping that he wouldn't mind. She needn't have worried.

He waved a hand at her mom. "Aww, shucks. You'll go giving me a big head."

Her mom smiled. "I can already tell that you're not one to do that. Have a seat. You've worked hard getting that thing in here."

He sat on the sofa, and Abbie shooed her mom to the chair by the fire. "You sit down, too." She gave them both their drinks and then offered the cookies around.

"Mmm." Ivan groaned as he bit into his. "You have to tell me where to get these. They're amazing. Are they from the bakery?"

Her mom laughed. "Good-looking, a gentleman, and smart, too? You just keep getting better."

He frowned. "You mean I guessed right? They're from the bakery?"

"No," said Abbie. "She thinks I must have told you that she bakes her own cookies and that you're smart for flattering her."

"Oh!" He grinned. "If I'd known, that's exactly what I would have done. But ..." He grinned at his cookie. "I had no idea, and it's the best cookie I've ever had."

Her mom smiled at him. "Flattery will get you a long way with me. I'll be baking all the time between now and Christmas, so I hope you'll keep coming back for more."

He smiled at Abbie. "You won't be able to keep me away."

Abbie laughed. "Now, I'll never know if it's me you want or just the cookies."

"I think we all know the answer to that one," said her mom.

Ivan nodded happily.

It felt strange to Abbie, but strange in a good way that now, they did all know that Ivan was here because he wanted to be with her—and that he wasn't afraid to make that known. She cast a glance at him and then at her mom, and at that moment, she decided that she needed to be as honest as he was being.

It was dark by the time Ivan got home. He wasn't a fan of the cold, short days at this time of year. He pulled into the garage, grateful that all the lights came on automatically both around and inside the house.

He opened the door to the kitchen and stopped as the light flickered on. Everyone kept getting after him about making this place more like a home. Maybe he should take a leaf out of Abbie's book and decorate for Christmas. He could get a tree, maybe ask her to go back to the lot with him next weekend. He smiled, liking that idea. He'd run it by her later.

He'd come home because he'd felt that she and her mom needed some time alone. Her mom had acted all bright and happy—and he didn't doubt that she was happy to have him around. But there was an undercurrent of sadness, too. She'd smiled a lot, but her eyes were a little too bright at times. He figured that she and Abbie needed to decorate their tree without him there. Even if he hoped he might become a part of their little family unit over time—and if he was honest, that was exactly what he was starting to want—he knew they needed to share their memories and their sadness by themselves.

Abbie had said she might come by tonight. Her mom had insisted that she should—she'd even threatened to get her sewing machine and country music out again. That had made him laugh. She knew her daughter well. But Abbie knew her, too, and when she'd walked Ivan to his car when he left, she'd told him that she'd need to play it by ear. Decorating the tree would be hard on her mom, and she might not want to leave her alone later.

He went through to the living room and smiled at the picture on the wall. He wouldn't ever have picked it out, but it went well with the décor. It was a photo of a storm over the ocean, with the sun shining just above the horizon. He liked the way the colors looked, but more than that, he liked the way it made him feel. The sun peeking out after a storm gave him hope.

His storms were a long way behind him these days, and he was ready for a new beginning.

His cell phone rang in his back pocket, and he pulled it out. He grimaced when he saw Neil's name on the display. Damn. He felt bad. How was Neil going to feel when he learned about him and Abbie? By the sounds of it, he wouldn't be too upset that she was seeing someone else. But that wasn't the point. The point was that Ivan had helped him get prepared for his date with her, and now he was the one seeing her. He stared at the name on the screen, feeling like an asshole. He should answer, but he didn't know what to say—and he couldn't not say anything.

It stopped ringing, and he waited, hoping that Neil would leave him a message. After a few moments, it beeped, indicating that he had.

Ivan blew out a sigh and hit the button, wondering what he was going to hear.

"Hi, Ivan. It's Neil. I know I said I'd call you on Saturday and let you know how my date went. But it didn't work out the way I expected. I feel pretty dumb, to be honest. I … I don't know. I guess I'll see you at work tomorrow. There's no need to call me back if you get this. I hope you've had a good weekend. Bye."

Ivan nodded to himself as he hung up. Of course. Tomorrow at work would be soon enough to explain himself. He wasn't worried about Neil being mad at him. He just felt like an asshole. He'd helped Neil figure out what to wear on the date, and then he'd gone out with Abbie—had sex with her—the very next day. That wasn't something a friend did, and he knew that Neil saw him as a friend—the only friend he'd made here. All he could do was be honest with the guy. If he and Abbie had hit it off, he would have respected that. He'd only been trying to respect what she said she wanted.

He went and stood in front of the windows and looked out into the darkness. He'd have to talk to Abbie later, whether she came over or not. He wanted to know more about this girl who Neil liked. Maybe he could help him get a date with her instead.

~ ~ ~

Abbie stood back and looked at the tree. "It's beautiful, Mom."

Her mom smiled. "It is. We did a good job of it."

"Are you okay?"

"I am, love. You know what I'm thinking."

"Of course, I do." Abbie sniffed. She'd been trying not to cry herself. When she was a little kid, the three of them had always decorated the tree together. In the last few years, before her dad died, she hadn't been home to do it with them. She supposed that was normal. Kids grew up and moved away and weren't there for all the little moments like that. But still … she wished that she'd gotten to share even just one more Christmas with them both. She could come home because her dad had died—why hadn't she been smart enough to come home and enjoy the time with him while he was still here?

Her mom came and wrapped her in a hug. "Don't look like that. He loved you."

Abbie nodded, determined not to cry. "I just wish …"

"We can wish all we want, Abbs, it doesn't change anything; it only makes us feel worse. I wish a lot of things, too, but it's better to focus on the good things."

"What's good about any of it? He's gone."

"It only hurts so much because we loved him so much. Instead of being sad that we don't have that anymore, we need to be grateful that we had him at all. I had the best husband I could ever have hoped for. You had the best dad. A lot of people don't ever get to know that kind of love in their lives. Yes, it was cut short, but we were lucky to have him at all. I try to be grateful for that. I try to focus on that."

Abbie stood back and wiped her eyes. "You're so strong, Mom."

Her mom gave her a sad smile. "Only because I don't have any choice. I wasn't strong in the beginning; I was falling apart. But you held me together. Now, all we can do is make the most of what is. And for you, that happens to be a very sweet and good-looking guy who's sitting at home right now, wondering if he'll get to see you again tonight."

Abbie smiled. Ivan had been so sweet—so understanding.

"I think you should go over there."

"No, I want to be here with you."

"Thanks, but I need to be by myself, Abbs."

"Are you just saying that because you want me to go and see Ivan? You don't need to worry, you know. He understands."

"I'm not just saying it. It's what I want. I want to be with my memories, and I want you to go and make some new memories with your new man."

"But …"

Her mom held up a hand. "Are you telling me you don't want him to be your man?"

She shook her head slowly. She'd decided she was going to be honest with Ivan and her mom about the way she felt. "No. That's what I'm hoping for. But I want to be with you while you're sad—while I'm sad."

"I know, but I think you should let him be there for you while you're sad. He wants to be. So, let him. If you close him out of the real stuff and only let him in for the fun stuff, that's not letting him be your man; that's just making him another guy you date."

Abbie held her gaze for a long moment, wanting to argue, but knowing she was right.

"Go on. Go see him and remember, I don't expect you home."

Abbie smiled. "I'll be home. I have work in the morning."

She pulled up outside Ivan's house and looked around as the lights came on over the front door. It opened, and he came out to greet her.

He reached the car as she opened the door and greeted her with a hug.

She clung to him for a moment, understanding the truth of what her mom had said. If she'd stayed home tonight, she would have had to be the strong one, being there for her mom. Her mom insisted that wasn't what she wanted, and now Ivan was being the strong one for her.

"Are you okay?" he asked. "Was that rough?"

"It was bittersweet. We cried, of course. But Mom's doing her best to find the positives. She told me it only hurts so much because we loved him so much."

"She's a smart lady, your mom. Come on in."

He took her coat in the hallway and hung it in the closet.

"Do you realize you've never told me about your family?" Abbie asked with a frown. "We've spent so much time talking about me and my mom and dad, what about you?"

He shrugged. "My parents are both gone."

"I'm sorry."

He shrugged again. "Thanks. That's why I said your mom's a smart lady. It's different for me. The two of you hurt so much over your dad because you loved him so much—and he loved you. It wasn't like that for me. My dad was hardly ever around when I was a kid. I think he's dead; that's what I heard. My mom died twelve years ago while I was in the army. I hadn't seen her in a couple of years before that."

"Wow." Abbie couldn't imagine what that must have been like. She'd drifted away from her parents, but nothing like that.

He smiled. "It is what it is. In a way, you're lucky to hurt the way you do over your dad because it means you lost something wonderful."

She gave him a half smile. She could see the logic—especially coming from his point of view, but she didn't think she'd ever believe she was lucky to have lost her dad.

"Anyway. Come on through. Do you want a drink?"

"Do you have any juice or soda? I don't want anything stronger than that."

He chuckled as he opened the fridge. "You don't want me getting you tipsy and taking advantage?"

She laughed. "I don't need to be tipsy for that—I was planning on taking advantage of you. It's just that I have work in the morning. Mondays are busy, and I need a clear head."

His smile disappeared as he poured two glasses of apple juice.

"What's wrong?"

"Just talking about work tomorrow."

"I thought you loved your job."

"I do. It's just that Neil left me a message a little while ago. He wanted to tell me how his date turned out. He said he'll tell me all about it tomorrow. I feel like a shit. I'll have to tell him that I already know—and that I've been seeing you all weekend."

Abbie's heart sank. "God. I'm horrible. I didn't even think. That's an awful situation—for you and for him. And I'm the one who caused it."

"You are not horrible! It's just the way things worked out. I could have told him that I didn't want to help him because I liked you myself—I could have been honest, but instead, I kept my mouth shut."

"But only because you were respecting what I said I wanted."

He gave her a rueful smile. "Yeah, even though I knew you were being a fool."

She laughed. "You did, huh?"

He nodded. "You'd have to be a fool to turn me down when it's so obvious that we're meant to be."

Her heart hammered in her chest.

"You told me yourself; we're the same kind of animal."

She looked up into his eyes. "You really think we're meant to be?"

He lowered his head until his lips were almost touching hers. "I want to. Do you?"

She nodded as her chest filled with warmth. "I want to."

This kiss was different. It filled her with longing for him, as his kisses always did, but it was gentler, more tender. It gave her hope that there was so much more to explore between them than what they could discover in bed.

When he finally lifted his head, she reached up and touched his cheek.

"I think we're onto something here, Abbie."

She smiled. She did, too.

His phone rang, and they both started. He made a face. "Damn. I hope that's not Neil again."

She felt bad.

He looked at the display and shook his head. "It's Colt. I can call him back tomorrow."

When it had stopped ringing, she reached up and kissed his lips. "Maybe you should call him back now. I have a call I need to make myself."

He frowned. "Right now?"

"Yeah. I should be the one to tell Neil about you and me. You shouldn't have to deal with that when you get to work tomorrow."

"It's okay."

"No, you said you feel bad about it. You shouldn't have to. That whole thing was my fault, and I need to be the one to make it right. I'll tell him." She smiled. "And maybe I'll offer to put a good word in for him with the girl at the library."

"If you're sure."

"I am. I feel like I'm finally ready to start getting things right, and that means fixing my screw-ups in the right way—instead of making things worse like I was doing before. You call Colt. I'm going to call Neil."

# Chapter Fourteen

Ivan was edgy when he got to work on Monday morning. Abbie had told him that Neil was cool. Apparently, he'd even told Abbie that he could see her being with Ivan much more easily than he could ever see her being with him.

Still, he couldn't help feeling ill at ease as he unlocked the office and turned the lights on. Abbie had wanted to be the one to talk to Neil—since she was the one who'd gone out with him. And Ivan understood that. He appreciated that she was trying to make up for her mistakes. But part of him still wished that he'd talked to Neil, man to man. Oh well. He'd talk to him when he came in, and then hopefully, it'd all be behind them.

He went into his office and booted up his computer then went to the break room to start the coffee.

He turned at the sound of Neil clearing his throat behind him.

"Oh. Hi. You're early."

Neil nodded. "Morning. I wanted a word."

Ivan's heart sank. He probably wanted to tell him he was a shit.

"Sure. The coffee will be ready in a minute. Fire away. I deserve it."

Neil looked puzzled. "You sound as though I'm going to be mad at you."

"You aren't?"

"No. I wanted to thank you. I had no idea that you liked Abbie. I would never have asked her out if I'd known."

"I should have said something, but she told me she wasn't interested. And she was interested in you."

Neil came in and sat down at the table. "She wasn't, though, was she? Just like I wasn't really interested in her. I'm glad she called me last night. She said you wanted to talk to me yourself, but it was better that she and I spoke. I don't think I would have been able to admit to you—or to myself if I were talking to you—that on some level, I knew you were the one she liked. I even tried to dress like you."

"I shouldn't have let you do that."

Neil laughed. "I didn't give you much choice. I asked you to help me and then told you exactly what I wanted. I wanted to look like you, be cool like you."

Ivan blew out a sigh. He didn't exactly think of himself as cool.

"It's okay. Abbie and I both learned something important from the whole experience."

Ivan raised an eyebrow.

"If you think about it, she was trying to be someone else just as much as I was."

Ivan didn't need to think about it. He remembered the way she'd been dressed on Friday night—he'd thought she was a middle-aged woman.

"She thought she needed to be with someone like me and tried to dress in a way she thought I'd like. Just the same as I did. That helped us both see that we wouldn't be happy if we weren't ourselves."

Ivan nodded.

"It's true for all of us. If we have to change who we are so that someone else will like us—it will never work. Instead of me dressing like you and Abbie dressing like Merry, it's better if we're all honest and go for the people we really like."

Ivan frowned. "I understand Abbie's reasons. She thought she needed to be with someone like you—someone dependable and responsible, with a good job and great prospects. Do you mind if I ask what your reasoning was?"

Neil shrugged. "I thought I wanted to be one of the cool kids. You know? I've always felt like I was on the outside looking in. Not quite cool enough, not quite good enough. I thought if someone like Abbie wanted to go out with me, that would show that I was good enough."

Ivan shook his head. "You're good enough just the way you are."

"I know, but it doesn't always feel that way."

"What if I told you that Abbie felt the same way—that if someone like you wanted to go out with her, that would show that she was good enough."

Neil smiled. "You don't need to tell me that; she already told me herself. I had no idea. It seems we were both way off the mark. But more importantly, we helped each other figure something out."

"Yeah?"

Neil nodded. "Maybe I shouldn't tell you this. Maybe I should let her tell you herself, but maybe she won't, so … You see, I know Merry is my kind of person. Abbie knew you were her kind of person. But we both have self-esteem issues. If we're not good enough—and you're just like us, then maybe someone very different would be better."

Ivan frowned.

"I thought I'd be cooler if I went out with Abbie. But cool doesn't do much for me. Abbie thought I was the more sensible choice—but sensible doesn't do much for her."

"I can see that."

Neil smiled. "So, now it's all sorted out. Everyone's happy. No hard feelings."

"Thanks. But wait … Abbie and I got together, that's all good, but what about you and Merry?"

Neil gave him a rueful smile. "That's the downside of being me. I'm still too scared to ask her out. What if she says no?"

"How can she say yes if you never ask?"

Neil shrugged.

"You should ask her."

"I need to get up the nerve first."

"The longer you think about it, the less likely it is to happen."

"Morning."

They both turned when Allie came in.

"Morning."

"How was your weekend?"

"Good, thanks. How about you?" asked Ivan.

Neil smirked at him and edged his way to the door. He usually removed himself when social chit-chat started up, but Ivan knew that he was wriggling out of having to commit to asking Merry out.

~ ~ ~

Abbie checked her watch. It was almost time to go for lunch, and she wanted to get out on time. She needed to run over to the women's center. That place had been a godsend when she first came back. Renée and the team of women who ran the place had helped her so much. From dealing with all the legal side of her dad's estate while her mom was still a mess, to helping her figure out payment plans to pay off their debt, they'd helped her with everything.

The woman she'd worked with most was Chris. In the last few months, she'd tried to encourage Abbie to leave the lake and let her mom stand on her own two feet. Abbie hadn't seen her in a while, but she needed to thank her. She was the one who'd put Abbie onto the job here. She didn't know what Chris wanted to see her about, but she was looking forward to telling her how things were going—and admitting that she could now understand what Chris had been telling her the whole time about not trying to become someone else in some attempt to make up for her past.

"Has he been through yet?"

She looked up when Cassie popped her head out of her office. "No. He's not here yet."

Cassie made a face. "Damn. Will you buzz me when he comes and again when he goes in with Michael?"

"Sure." Abbie had to wonder what on earth Cassie's problem with Colt might be. She was adamant that she didn't want to run into him.

She raised an eyebrow at her. "Are you worried he's going to arrest you or something?"

Cassie made a face. "No. I just don't want to run into him. We have a lot of history, and none of it's good. I've managed to avoid him since I came back to town, and I'd like to keep it that way. Shit!"

Abbie followed her gaze to the outer door which Colt was about to come through. "You go back—" she started to tell Cassie, but there was no need; her door had already closed.

"Hey, Abbie."

"Hi, Colt. Michael should be with you in a couple of minutes."

Colt took his hat off and held it in front of him. He looked like he was going to say something, but instead, went toward the chairs in the waiting room. Then, he turned around so fast he made Abbie jump. "Is Cassie around?"

You weren't supposed to lie to a police officer! Abbie frowned. "She's in her office." Hopefully, that implied that she was with a patient.

It was enough to persuade Colt to go and sit down with a muttered, "Thanks."

Now all Abbie had to do was hope that Michael didn't take too long. She needed him to come out and take Colt in for his appointment so that she could tell Cassie the coast was clear and then get out of here for her lunch!

To her relief, Michael came out a few minutes later and smiled at her. "Can you make Mr. Flynn an appointment for next week, Abbie?"

"I sure can."

"Thanks. Do you want to come through, Colt?"

Abbie made Mr. Flynn's appointment and then buzzed Cassie. "You're safe to come out."

Cassie popped her head around her door again, and Abbie laughed. "What is the deal with you two?"

Cassie rolled her eyes. "I told you, I don't want to run into him."

"Maybe so, but the Cassie Stevens I remember never hid from anyone."

Cassie shrugged. "Yeah, well, I'm older and wiser these days. Sometimes it's easier to take the path of least resistance."

"Dare I ask what's going on?"

"Nothing. Nothing at all. I just don't want to see him."

"Wait, didn't you two used to go out in high school?"

"Yup. But that was a long time ago."

"It didn't end well?"

Cassie let out a bitter little laugh. "Now, there's an understatement. Anyway, I need to get out of here before he comes out."

Abbie shot a glance at the clock. "I need to get out of here, too. I have an appointment."

"Just put the answering machine on. There are no more appointments until two."

"I have to wait for Colt to come out first."

"Buzz Michael and tell him you need to go. He won't mind."

Abbie hesitated. "No. I'll hang on a few minutes."

Cassie shrugged. "Your choice, but I'm not waiting with you."

Abbie chuckled. "Go on, then, get out while the going's good."

Cassie stopped when she reached the door. "I'm not being a coward, you know."

"I didn't say you were."

"Good. It's just that some things are better left in the past, you know?"

"Whatever you say."

Cassie gave her a weird look and then left.

Abbie looked up at the clock again. She really needed to get out of here soon if she wasn't going to be late for Chris.

She managed to get there just on time. Chris greeted her in the bakery with a smile. "Hi, Abbie. How are you?"

"I'm good, thanks. How are you?"

Chris smiled. "Everything's rosy in my garden. Come on in. I know you're on your lunch break, so I won't keep you long."

Abbie followed her into the office where they'd had so many meetings over the last year. Chris had been good to her. She'd felt like the only person in the world she had to turn to sometimes.

"How've you been?"

"Good, thanks. What's up?"

Chris laughed. "Always one to get to the point. There's nothing wrong. In fact, there might be something very right. I heard about a job you might like."

Abbie frowned. "I'm at the medical center."

"I know, but it's not exactly your dream job, is it?"

"I don't have one. I just need to make enough money to get by."

Chris shook her head. "That was just the first step. First, you find your feet, then you can look to grow from there."

"I suppose." It always seemed that Chris had higher hopes for her than she did for herself.

"There's only one thing, though."

Abbie had a feeling she knew what was coming.

"The job's in San Francisco."

"Then, I'm out. It doesn't matter what the job is. You know that, Chris."

"I do, but I had to ask. Your mom's doing so much better now. She can cope—financially and otherwise."

"She can. But that's not the point. I want to be here with her." They'd had this discussion so many times. Abbie had had the feeling in the past that Chris and her mom may have talked and were trying to get her to put her own interests first. She knew her mom wouldn't have had anything to do with this, though. Not now. She smiled, knowing that now she'd be able to persuade Chris that she had her own reasons for wanting to stay at the lake. "And besides, I want to stay for me, too."

Chris raised an eyebrow. "Why's that?"

"I met someone."

Chris's reaction surprised her. She didn't look impressed.

"You'd like him, Chris. He's good for me—good to me. It's only early days yet, but I have high hopes."

Chris sighed. "We've talked about his before, Abbie. I heard you were out with Neil on Friday. Do you really think that you and he—"

"No!" Abbie laughed. "You heard about that? Damn. You can't get away with anything around here. That was a mistake, but I can't regret it, because it helped me finally get my head on straight. Neil's a sweetheart, but he's not for me."

Chris frowned. "So, who are you talking about?"

"Ivan … he works for …"

Chris clapped her hands together with a smile. "Ivan? I know who he works for!"

"Oh, of course." Chris was now engaged to Seymour Davenport—Ivan's boss.

"Oh, Abbie! That's perfect."

Abbie grinned. "I think so."

"Oh, I know so. He's wonderful. And so are you. I know you wanted to find someone like Neil, but Abbie, that wouldn't suit you; you'd be miserable even if you did make it work somehow."

"I know. I already figured that out."

"I'm glad. So, I don't need to try to get you out of town before you make a horrible mistake with Neil?"

"Is that what you were trying to do?"

"I'm afraid so. You were dead set on settling down last time we talked. I knew I couldn't talk you out of it, so I thought maybe I could offer you something that appealed more."

"Even if it were the best job in the world, I wouldn't have left my mom."

Chris's smile faded. "Does she know about Ivan?"

Abbie laughed. "Not only does she know, she loves him. And he likes her, too."

"That's great. I'm not going to say anything else. It looks like you have it all figured out for yourself." She stood up. "I'll let you get back to work."

"Thanks." Abbie hugged her. "I wouldn't have been able to get through this last year without you, you know."

Chris hugged her back. "Yes, you would. You would have done just fine. And you'll do fine going forward, too. But remember, I'll be here for you if ever you need me."

"Thanks."

~ ~ ~

Ivan looked up at the sound of a knock on his office door. "Come in." He didn't normally keep the door closed, but he'd had a lot of work to get through this afternoon, and he didn't need any interruptions.

He was surprised to see Seymour Davenport standing there. "Oh, hi."

"Hey. I don't need to interrupt if you're busy."

"It's fine. What's happening?"

Mr. D smiled. "It's not a business call; it's personal." He closed the door behind him. "I can come back another time if that'd be better."

It would be better, workwise, but Mr. D hadn't ever come to see him at the office on a personal matter before. Ivan wasn't about to send him away. "Now's good. What's going on?"

"That's what I came to ask you. I worried about you all weekend. I kept wondering how you were doing. This morning, I learned that my nephew is looking for someone to help run his community center in LA. The job description sounded like he was describing you. I wondered if that might appeal to you."

Ivan frowned. "Am I not doing a good job here?"

"You're doing wonderfully. I'd hate to lose you. I'm trying not to be selfish. I'm concerned about you."

"Why?"

"Because I landed you in this small town where your only dating options aren't suitable ones."

Ivan had to laugh. "You're still worried that I was interested in a girl who was going out with Neil?"

Mr. D nodded. "Exactly! It worried me."

Ivan laughed again. "Then worry no more. She wasn't Neil's type. He wasn't hers. She and I spent most of the weekend together. And before you ask, Neil knows and is happy about it, and we're going to try to fix him up with a girl he really likes."

Mr. D frowned. "Part of me wants to ask, what the hell? But the rest of me knows better. So, it all worked out?"

"Better than I ever dreamed."

"But …"

Ivan smiled. "You'll understand when you meet her. You'll get it."

"Okay. As long as you're happy, I'm happy. So, I can tell Oscar that I don't have a candidate for the job, after all?"

"Please do. I'm happy here."

"I'm glad to hear it." He smiled. "Would you and your young lady like to have dinner with Chris and me sometime?"

Ivan smiled. "I'd love to. I'll ask her."

"Good. I'll look forward to it." Mr. D chuckled. "And could you also ask her to do something about decorating your place?"

Ivan laughed. "Yeah. I think I'm going to ask her to help me decorate for Christmas this weekend.

# Chapter Fifteen

When Abbie got to work on Wednesday morning, she checked over the list of appointments. It looked like it'd be a quiet day. She made a face when she saw Colt's name on the list. She'd have to make sure that she warned Cassie. Maybe she'd get her to tell her why she was so intent on avoiding him.

"G'morning, Abbs."

"Hey, Michael."

"Listen, Megan's going to pop in this morning, around ten-thirty. Can you buzz me when she gets here? I'll stick my head out for a minute. I need a word with her."

"Of course. Is she off today?"

"Yeah. She's up to something." He grinned. "I don't know what, but I'm guessing she might be getting my Christmas present. See if you can find out?"

Abbie laughed. "No way! I'm not spilling her secrets."

He shrugged. "I'll get it out of her. Oh, and do you want to come over to the house on Friday? She wants to have a few people over."

"Can I let you know?" Abbie didn't know what her plans were for the weekend, but she didn't want to commit to anything that didn't include Ivan.

"Sure, it's nothing formal or anything. Just drop by if you like. She's invited the gang and the people from work."

That got Abbie's attention. "Oh. Is Merry going?"

"Yeah, do you know her? If you do, please come. I can never get a word out of her."

"I don't know her."

"That figures. I don't think she knows anyone. We need to get her out and meeting people."

Abbie grinned. "I do know that there's someone who'd like to meet her."

Michael came out into the reception area and leaned on the desk. "A guy?"

"Yes."

He made a face. "I'm not sure she'd go for that. I think she'd probably run and hide. I thought Meggie was shy. Merry's even quieter. Who is this guy anyway?"

"Neil. He works with Ivan."

Michael raised an eyebrow. "You know what gossip's like around here. Neil's the guy you were out with last Friday?"

Abbie sighed. "Yes. The guy I should never have gone out with. But he's nice. He's an accountant. And he has a crush on Merry."

Michael grinned. "This sounds promising. Do you know him well enough to invite him to our place on Friday?"

Abbie grinned back. "I think I can get him there."

"Awesome!" He looked up as Cassie came in. "Good morning, Doctor Stevens, and how are you this fine day?"

Cassie gave him a wary look. "I'm fine, thank you. At least, I was until I saw that smile on your face. What are you up to? I know when you're scheming, and right now, I'm worried."

Michael laughed. "You got me. I am scheming. But you're safe, for now. I'm just trying to set up Megan's assistant with a friend of Abbie's." He winked at her. "Even I'm not dumb enough to think I could do any matchmaking for you."

"Good. I told you when you invited me back here; I love Summer Lake, and there's only one thing that could make me change my mind about coming back."

"I know, darl'. I wouldn't dream of interfering there."

Abbie raised an eyebrow. "Does anyone want to fill me in?"

Cassie gave her a sour look. "Want to? No. But I will. Remember, I didn't want to run into Colt?"

"Oh."

"Yeah. I need to tell you …" Michael looked uneasy.

"What?"

"He's coming back in this morning."

Cassie pressed her lips together. "What time?"

"Ten-forty-five," said Abbie.

"Okay. Well, we can do the same as we did on Monday, right?"

Abbie nodded.

"Anyway. Let's leave that subject alone, shall we? Is this some kind of meeting I need to be in on, or can I get into my office and get set up for the day?"

"Go ahead," said Michael. "We're just talking social stuff. Are you coming on Friday?"

"Is Colt?"

Michael laughed. "I value my life more than that!"

"Then, maybe."

The morning soon got busy, and before Abbie knew it, it was ten-thirty. She smiled when she saw Megan come in, carrying little Billy.

"Hi, Abbie. You don't need to disturb him; he said he'd leave some things out here with you."

Abbie held up a bag Michael had left on the reception desk. "He did, but he asked me to buzz him when you came in; said he wanted a word."

"Okay, then, but I can wait until his patient comes out. I don't like to interrupt."

Megan was a sweetheart. Abbie liked her a lot, and she was glad to get a few minutes with her while she waited. "Do you mind if I ask you about Merry?"

"What about her?" Megan sat Billy up on the counter, and he waved a pudgy little hand at Abbie. He was adorable.

"I know someone who likes her. I'd like to help set them up, but I don't know her, and I don't know how to go about it."

Megan smiled. "I don't think there's much point. She doesn't go out. I've invited her over on Friday, but I don't think she'll come. Are you coming?"

"I don't know yet."

"I hope you can, but no worries if you can't. But Merry? Even if I could get her there, I don't think you'd have much of a chance of introducing her to someone. She already has this huge crush on a guy. I doubt she'll ever do anything about it, though."

Aww. Abbie felt bad for Neil. She'd been hoping that she'd be able to help him and Merry on their way. "Who is he?"

"His name's Neil. You might know him. He works for Seymour Davenport."

Abbie laughed out loud, making Billy turn to stare and then laugh with her.

"What's so funny?" asked Megan.

"Not only do I know him, but he's the guy I want to set her up with. He has a huge crush on her, too!"

"Oh, my goodness! That's perfect! We need to get them together somehow."

Michael's door opened, and Mr. Johnson came out. Abbie buzzed Michael to let him know that Megan was here.

Michael came out, and Billy squealed. "Daddy!" Michael scooped him off the counter and swung him around, then handed him, giggling, to Abbie.

"Can you watch the little guy for a minute?"

Abbie nodded. She wasn't sure about being left alone with a small boy, but Michael and Megan seemed to have faith in her, even if she didn't. They disappeared into Michael's office.

Billy smiled at her and pulled a strand of her hair. "Abbie," he said with a smile.

"That's right."

She looked up when the door opened, and Colt came in.

Crap! She needed to warn Cassie not to come out.

"Hey, little mister!" Colt came straight to Billy. "How's it going?" He held a hand up, and Billy high-fived him.

"If you want to take a seat, Michael should be out in a minute."

"That's okay. I'll hang with my little buddy here."

Abbie wished he'd go and sit down so she could buzz Cassie without him hearing.

Billy grinned at him. "Sherf!"

Colt laughed. "You remembered! Sheriff!" He grinned at Abbie. "Michael was trying to teach him—" His smile disappeared as he looked over her shoulder, and Abbie knew who he'd seen.

She turned around with an apologetic look. Mrs. Thomson walked out with a smile, and Cassie stood frozen to the spot. She looked as if she'd seen a ghost.

To Abbie's relief, Michael's door opened, and he and Megan came out. For a moment, they all froze. Billy broke the silence when he shouted, "Daddee!" and lunged toward Michael.

Abbie hung on tight, afraid to drop him.

Michael came to her. "Billy!" He took him from her arms. "And your friend, the sheriff. Why don't you two come in with me?"

He went to Colt and thrust Billy into his arms. That was enough to break the spell, and Colt took the kid and followed Michael into his office.

"I'm so sorry, Cassie!"

She shook her head. "It's fine. It's not a problem." The look on her face said it was, but she gave them a forced smile. "Is Mrs. Morton here?"

"Not yet."

"Okay. Give me a buzz when she arrives." She went back into her office and closed the door behind her.

Abbie let out a big sigh. "Damn. I blew that."

Megan patted her arm. "Don't worry about it. It's not your place to run interference for her."

"I don't mind. I want to help her out. I don't even know what her problem is, though. Do you?"

Megan nodded. "I do. They need to work it out at some point. But, to be honest, I don't know how they can." She looked at Michael's door. "I hope it's not going to be like this all the time, though. It affects the rest of us. You feel bad that you didn't warn her he was here, and now I have to wait around until I can get Billy back."

"Yeah, but she's not doing it on purpose."

"No, I know. But we all need to sort our personal problems out before they start affecting other people."

~ ~ ~

Ivan smiled as he hung up the phone. That was the first time Abbie had called him at work. He'd told her she could call any time, but up until now, they'd only talked and seen each other after work. That wasn't the only reason he was smiling. She'd asked him if he wanted to go out on Friday night, and explained that they had a chance to get Neil and Merry together.

He got up from his desk. Time to go see if Neil was up for it.

Neil gave him a wary look when he reached his office. "What is it?"

Ivan grinned. "I have some good news for you."

"What?"

"You're coming out on Friday."

"I am? Why? Where are we going?"

"To Michael and Megan's place, for a little get-together."

Neil sucked in a deep breath. "Megan, who works at the library?"

"Yep, and you're the accountant, so I reckon you can put two and two together and come up with the answer to who else is going to be there."

Neil nodded slowly.

"Come on. Smile. This is your big chance!"

"But what if I blow it?"

Ivan grinned. "You won't."

"You don't know that. She might think I'm awful."

"She doesn't."

"But you … wait, what? What makes you say that?"

"I just talked to Abbie, who just talked to Megan, who told her that Merry is going to be there on Friday, but there was no point trying to introduce her to a guy because she already has this huge crush."

Neil looked so disappointed that he felt bad drawing it out like this.

"On some guy named Neil—an accountant who goes in the library sometimes but only ever talks to her about books."

Neil's eyes grew wide. "She has a crush on me?"

Ivan nodded happily. "There you were telling me that she didn't know you existed, and all this time, she's been pining for you."

"Wow! Oh, my God! That's … I don't know what to say."

"Say that you're coming on Friday."

"I am. I will. I'll be there. I … what should I wear?" He laughed. "Actually, forget I asked that. I've learned my lesson. If she likes me, then she likes me as I am."

"Exactly."

Neil grinned. "I don't know how to thank you."

"You don't need to. It all worked out in the end."

"It hasn't yet."

"It will. We'll make sure of it."

When he got back to his office, Ivan sat there, smiling to himself. Everything was working out. He was happier than he remembered being in a long time—if ever. He'd lived a solitary life for such a long time. He hadn't thought he wanted friends or a girl in his life. Now he had both, and he was loving it. He picked his phone up. He'd not long ago spoken to Abbie, but he wanted to hear her voice again.

"Summer Lake Medical Center, this is Abbie, how can I help you?"

"You can have dinner with me tonight."

"Oh. Hey. Did you tell him?"

"I did. He's thrilled. But I'm more interested in you and me. Will you have dinner with me tonight?"

"Okay."

"Thanks. I'll come pick you at seven."

"I can drive myself."

"I don't like you driving home so late afterward, and it's supposed to snow again tonight."

She was quiet for a long moment, and he wondered if she was going to argue. Instead, she made his heart beat faster. "I was thinking I could stay. Then I can drive straight to work in the morning."

"Great."

"Okay. I'll see you just after seven. I have to go."

"See you later." He wanted to say something more than that, wanted to tell her he couldn't wait, that she meant a lot to him. He hung up and stared out the window for a long moment, realizing what he really wanted to say. Maybe it was just because people said those three words at the end of a phone call—or maybe it was because they were true?

He shook his head. It was way too soon to be saying that. They'd only been seeing each other a couple of weeks. He blew out a sigh. Everything else in his life had happened so fast—moving here to the lake, starting his new job, living in the house. Was it possible that he could fall for her just as fast? That once he'd figured out that he wanted to be with her, he'd let all his defenses down and let her into his heart? The way his heart was beating, as though it was trying to escape his ribcage, told him that it might be true.

He'd need to be very careful before he said those three words out loud. Even if they were true, how long would it take before they were even a possibility for Abbie? He didn't want to scare her away by asking too much of her too soon.

He turned back to his computer. Maybe tonight he should test the waters somehow. She'd talked about settling down and getting married and all that stuff when she'd been convinced that that was the kind of life she ought to be living. She'd never mentioned that she actually wanted it, and she certainly hadn't ever mentioned falling in love.

He blew out a sigh. Maybe he was crazy? Maybe he needed to slow down and play the waiting game—see where things went with time. Or maybe, just maybe, he needed to let her know how he was starting to feel so they could figure it out between them.

He shrugged. It was too big a question to answer right now, and besides, he had work to do. He could face it later when he saw her.

~ ~ ~

"Are you sure you don't mind?"

Abbie's mom rolled her eyes. "How many times do I have to say it? I'm fine. I'd rather you stayed at Ivan's than stay here. I want you to go. I want you to get on with your life, and I need you to let me figure out how to get on with mine."

Abbie frowned. "I need to let you?"

"Yes, Abbs. I don't want you to think I'm not grateful, but it's time. You got me through the worst, and I love you for it. But as much as you need to get on with your life, I need to get on with mine. Depending on you for everything isn't doing me any good."

"What do you want to do?"

"I don't know. I need to find a better job for starters."

Abbie nodded. She'd lost her job after Abbie's dad had died. For a long time, she hadn't been up to doing much. But over the summer, she'd worked on the cleaning crew at the resort. As one of the last in, she'd been the first out when the busy season ended. Ben, who owned the resort, had given her whatever hours he could in housekeeping, but she was only a backup.

"I've been thinking about going to the women's center and asking for help."

Abbie didn't know what to say. Part of her wanted to say she didn't need to do that. That she could take care of her. But she understood what her mom was saying.

"I'm not an old lady, Abbs. I don't want to be dependent on you anymore. For your sake or mine."

"Do you have any idea what you do want?"

Her mom smiled. "What I want right now is for you to get going. Have a lovely evening with Ivan. Say hello to him for me. Stay over there, and don't give me another thought. And then soon—maybe this weekend—I want to talk to you about what I should do from here on out."

"Do you want to—"

Her mom held up a hand. "I don't want to talk about it tonight. I want you to go and have fun. Can you do that for me?"

Abbie went to hug her. "I can."

"Good. And if you don't have any other plans, ask Ivan if he wants to come over on Sunday for lunch. I'll bake cookies."

Abbie laughed. "Then, I can already tell you that he'll say yes."

Her mom hugged her. "I have a good feeling about you two, Abbs."

Abbie squeezed her tight. "So do I."

# Chapter Sixteen

Ivan hurried out to the garage when he saw headlights coming up the driveway. He pushed the button so that the door opened and the lights came on, hoping that Abbie would take the hint and come and park inside.

She pulled her car up next to his and got out with a smile. "Hey."

He went to her and closed his arms around her. "Hello, beautiful. I missed you."

She laughed. "It's only been a couple of days, and we spoke earlier."

"I know, but I still missed you."

"Aww ..." She tightened her arms around his waist. "I'll make it up to you later."

He lowered his lips to hers. "You can start now."

Her arms came up around his shoulders, and she kissed him. He loved her kisses; she was bold and hungry for him. As he kissed her back, the rest of the world melted away. All that was left was the two of them.

When she eventually pulled back, she gave him a puzzled look. "Is everything okay?"

"Couldn't be better, now you're here."

She smiled. "That's the way I feel, too. It's like coming here, to you, is coming to my safe place, my happy place."

He nodded, glad that she felt that way. "That's what I want this place to be for you. I told you I'd help you chase the blues away."

"And you've succeeded."

"Come on in. Have you eaten?"

"No. I thought I was going to have dinner with Mom before I came over. But she said she was going out to eat." She frowned. "I'm a bit worried about her."

"Why?"

"Because she's really stepping up the whole wanting to do things by herself. I mean, that's great and everything, but …"

"You're worried that she's only doing it so you won't do so much for her?"

She nodded. "Yeah. I'm starting to feel guilty. Like she doesn't want to ask anything of me because she doesn't want to interfere with us."

Ivan had a feeling that might be the case, but at the same time, it might not be. "Do you think that maybe she's just ready to face life for herself again?"

Abbie frowned. "That's what she says, but I don't know …"

"Can you go off anything other than what she says?"

"I know I should take her at her word, but it scares me."

"Why?"

"Because …" She blew out a sigh. "I feel responsible for her."

"But you're not. She's your mom. She's her own person."

"I know. I just don't want to let her down again."

"You can't let her down if you're respecting her wishes."

"That's true. I just feel so guilty."

"About your dad?"

"Yes. That, and the fact that now I've met you, I have a happy place, a life." She hesitated and looked up into his eyes. "Maybe a future. Mom doesn't have any of that. I don't want her to feel like I came back for a while and then abandoned her again."

Ivan went to her and closed his arms around her. "You're not abandoning her, though. You're only doing what any normal person does. They spend some time with their family; they spend some time with their partner." He took a deep breath, knowing this was risky, but she'd just mentioned the possibility of them having a future. It wasn't so far-fetched for him to talk about what that future might look like. "It's not like being with me means you won't ever be with her. I'd like to include her, too. In fact, I wanted to ask if you both want to come for lunch on Sunday. I'm not a great cook, but I can smoke a mean prime rib."

Abbie looked up into his eyes and smiled. "You're so sweet. She asked if you wanted to come over to our house on Sunday—even said she'd bake cookies for you."

He smiled. "How about you come over here? Your mom can bake, and I'll make lunch."

"That sounds great. But what about me? What am I going to contribute?"

He tucked a strand of hair behind her ear. "You can just sit around and look beautiful."

She laughed. "Err, I don't think so."

"Actually, there is something I wanted to ask for your help with."

"What's that?"

"I want to decorate for Christmas."

She grinned. "Now, that is something I can do." Her smile faded. "Though I'm not sure it's something I want to do for you."

He raised an eyebrow. "No?"

"I mean, it's something I want to do with you. We should do that together. Having decorations is nice, but it's the putting them up that makes them special."

"I'll have to take your word for that."

"You'll see. We'll decorate this year, and we'll mess up, and stupid stuff will happen, and we'll laugh and then next year, we'll remember it all and—"

She stopped abruptly, and he knew what she was thinking. She didn't want to presume that they'd even be together next year. He hoped it was only a case of her not wanting to presume too much. Because he already knew that he wanted to spend next Christmas with her—and every Christmas after that. "And each year, we'll add another layer of memories and make our own little traditions, right?"

She nodded. "That's how it works."

He tucked his fingers under her chin and made her look up into his eyes. "That's how I want it to work for us, Abbs."

She searched his face. "You do?"

"Yeah. I do. I'm hoping this is just our first Christmas together."

"I'd like that." She slid her arms up around his neck and pulled him down into a kiss. He closed his eyes and held her close to his chest as he kissed her, hoping that she was his future.

When they finally came up for air, she cocked her head to one side. "I'm glad you told me that. There's something I've been wanting to tell you, and knowing that you feel that way makes it easier to say."

He frowned, wondering where she was going. She reached up and touched his cheek. "You might think this is crazy, but I promised myself after the Neil episode that I was going to be open and honest with myself and with you about how I really feel. So ..." She took a deep breath. "What I'm trying to say is—and it's okay if you don't feel the same way, I just need you to know ..."

The look in her eyes told him before she finally got the words out. By the time she said them, his heart was buzzing in his chest, because it had its answer—the answer it had been hoping for.

"I know it's too soon, but I love you, Ivan."

He tightened his arms around her. "Maybe it is too soon. But I love you, too, Abbie. I didn't want to push you."

She laughed. "I didn't want to push you. I didn't want you to think that I was ... I don't know, still screwing things up somehow. This isn't me thinking I'm supposed to be with someone. This is me falling for you because I can't help it. Right or wrong, you've worked your way into my heart."

"That makes me happy."

"What, that I didn't want to fall for you?"

He laughed. "Not that so much. But that even though you didn't plan to, you couldn't help it. I didn't plan to fall for you either, but ..." He shrugged. He didn't know how to put it into words. "I guess we're just meant to be. I didn't think I was ready to fall in love and settle down, but then you showed up, and all of a sudden, it's all I can think about."

She smiled. "My mom said something like that. She told me I shouldn't be trying to make decisions about where my life should go because it doesn't work that way. When the person you're supposed to be with shows up, it all just works out the way that it's supposed to."

"I like the sound of that. Are you ready for it?"

"I think I am. I'm ready for you and me. My hesitation is what I still need to do for my mom."

"I think that, too, will work out the way it's supposed to."

"I hope so."

Ivan did, too. He was thrilled that Abbie felt the same way he did—that they'd both spoken those three little words. He was filled with hope, but there was some trepidation. He was thinking about a future for Abbie and him. He wanted her mom to be a part of it—but not a central part. He understood Abbie's desire to take care of her, but he hoped that her desire to take care of herself was stronger.

Michael and Megan's house was gorgeous. It was just a little farther down Main Street from Ivan's place. Abbie looked around the living room. It might not be far away in distance, but it was a whole world away from Ivan's in the way it felt. This was a family home, there was no mistaking that fact. There were pictures of Michael and Megan and their two boys. There were shelves filled with books and toys. There were so many little touches that no designer would ever have put there, but that gave the place its warm and welcoming style.

Right now, it was filled with people, too. Cassie was standing in a corner, chatting to Renée and her husband, Gabe. Missy was sitting on the sofa chatting with Emma and Holly, while Michael was in the hallway with Jack and Pete. So many familiar faces, but Abbie was most interested in one she didn't know so well—Merry hadn't arrived yet.

"There you are!" Megan came toward her with a smile. "I was just telling Merry I wanted to introduce her to you." She frowned. "And to Ivan and his friend. Where is he?"

"He'll be along in a little while."

"Oh. Okay. Do you want to come into the kitchen where it's quieter? She's more comfortable in there."

"Oh, so that's where she is?"

"Yeah. I thought I was bad at meeting new people, but she's even worse. She doesn't want to come out here, so would you mind coming in there?"

"Sure. It looks like she and Neil are a perfect match."

"Why's that?"

"Ivan's gone over to his place to make sure he comes. It sounded like he was on the verge of chickening out."

Megan laughed. "I didn't even tell Merry he was coming. She probably would have locked herself in her house and not come out if she knew."

"Aww. I hope this isn't going to be too difficult for them."

Megan stopped at the kitchen door. "It's not like we're going to lock them in a room together. All we're doing is giving them the opportunity. It's up to them what they do with it—or if they do anything at all. Come on." She opened the kitchen door, and Abbie smiled at the girl who was standing there looking nervous.

"Merry, this is Abbie."

"Nice to meet you."

"You, too," said Abbie. "I'm glad you came."

"You are, why? I think I've seen in you the library, but we don't know each other."

"No, but I'd like to. I heard you haven't made many friends here yet."

"No. I'm not very good at that sort of thing, and to be honest …" She looked at Megan. "I don't think this is the best way for me to start. I know there are dozens of people out there, and I don't think I can do this. I need to go." She started toward the back door.

"Just stay a little while," said Megan.

"I can't. I'm sorry."

Abbie could see that the poor thing was in a panic. "If you're leaving, would you mind if I come with you?"

Merry gave her a puzzled look. "Why?"

"Well, because if a whole bunch of people is too much, maybe one on one would be better."

"Okay." Abbie was relieved to see her smile.

"What about Ivan?" asked Megan. Though Abbie knew she was really asking about Neil.

"I can call him, tell him I'll meet up with him later."

"Okay. I'll give you a call over the weekend, Merry."

"Thanks." She was very pretty when she smiled. The hostile vibe she'd been giving off at first was just nerves, Abbie was now sure.

They went out the back of the house, and it was only when the cold hit her that Abbie remembered her coat. "I need to go back for my coat; I'm guessing you left yours, too?"

"Yeah. I'm sorry. When I get like that, I just need to get away. Freezing on my way home is preferable to going back in there."

"That's okay. I'll go back in for them."

Inside, she grabbed her coat, and Megan gave her Merry's. She hurried back out and wasn't surprised that Merry was already shivering when she got there.

Once they were both bundled up, Abbie offered Merry her arm. "Where are we going?"

"I live at the end of Maple."

"Okay, want to link with me so we can keep each other from slipping?"

Merry slipped her arm through Abbie's and started walking. "You don't need to come with me, you know."

"I know, but don't you want to get to know me? I'm not that bad, I promise."

Merry shot her a sideways glance. "I didn't think you were."

"Good."

They walked in silence for a little while, and it reminded Abbie of her walk into town with Neil. It was awkward, but she didn't know how to make it any better. She slowed when they came in sight of Ivan's house and smiled when she saw his car in the driveway.

"Would you mind very much if we stop in to see a friend of mine? He lives just here."

"That's okay. You go and see him. I can get myself home."

Abbie frowned. She so wanted this to work out somehow. Then she remembered. She'd made a promise to herself that she was going to be open and honest with herself and everyone else. She wondered if that might work out now with Merry. There was only one way to find out. "I'd like you to come. I'd like to introduce you to him, and I think he has his friend with him."

Merry shook her head rapidly. "Thanks, but I don't think that's a good idea."

"What if I told you that his friend is Neil? And that he was bringing Neil to Megan's place because he wanted to see you."

Merry's cheeks flushed crimson. "Neil?"

Abbie nodded.

"He was coming to see me?"

She nodded again.

"Oh."

"What do you say?"

"I … I don't think I can."

"Sure, you can. It won't be a big crowd, not like at Megan's."

She shook her head. "I can barely talk to him when he comes into the library. There's no way I could do it with two strangers watching."

Abbie pulled out her phone. "Well, I need to tell Ivan that we're not at Megan's anymore. Should I tell him that you're going home and that Neil won't get to see you?"

Merry looked so torn it was almost comical.

"This is your chance if you want to take it."

Merry grimaced. "I want to, but I don't know if I can."

"Just dive in; be brave."

She blew out a sigh. "Okay. But if I run out the back door, just let me go?"

Abbie chuckled. "Can I at least come after you to give you a ride home?"

"Maybe."

Abbie dialed Ivan's number and waited.

"Hey, Abbs. We'll be there soon. Neil just needed a bit of time to steel his nerves. We're at my place."

Abbie grinned at Merry. "Oh, so he's nervous to the point of freaking out too?"

Merry's eyes widened at that.

"Yeah. Though he's more nervous about the house full of people than about Merry."

"Well. Merry didn't like the house full of people either. So, we're just outside your place. I was going to bring Merry in, but I thought I should warn you first."

Ivan chuckled. "Awesome. I'll tell him. See you in a minute. I'll open the gate."

As they walked up the driveway. Merry clutched at Abbie's arm. "I'm scared."

"Of what?"

"That I won't know what to say to him."

"You'll be fine. He's as nervous as you are. You'll get past it."

"I hope so."

They both looked up as the front door opened. They were still halfway down the drive, but Ivan grinned at her, and Neil looked scared to death. Abbie squeezed Merry's arm. "You can do this. You like him, right?"

She nodded.

"Well, he likes you, too. The logical thing to do is to talk to each other so you can find out if there's anything to this mutual attraction."

Merry finally smiled. "Thank you. You just said the magic word."

"I did? What?"

"Logic. I can do the logical thing—and my behavior so far hasn't been logical. In fact, it's been downright irrational. Now I can talk to him because it's the logical thing to do."

Abbie chuckled. "Awesome. Come on, then."

When they reached the house, Ivan smiled at Merry. "It's nice to finally meet you, Merry. I'm Ivan. I work with Neil, and I've heard a lot about you."

Neil shot him a panicked look, but Merry smiled. "It's nice to meet you, too. Thank you for this." She turned to Neil. "I was on my way home. Would you like to walk with me?"

He nodded rapidly. "I ... I ... Would you like to go to Giuseppe's for dinner?"

Abbie tensed, hoping that wasn't asking too much. To her relief, Merry nodded. "Yes. Yes, I would." She let go of Abbie's arm and smiled at her. "Thank you."

Abbie smiled back. "You are most welcome. I hope you have a lovely evening."

Neil smiled at them. "I believe we will. Shall we go?"

Merry nodded, and they walked away.

Abbie and Ivan exchanged a glance and then watched them go.

"Can you believe that?" asked Ivan once they were out of earshot.

Abbie laughed. "I wouldn't if I hadn't seen it with my own eyes."

Ivan laughed with her. "Well, we did our bit. It's up to them what they do with it from here."

"I think it might just work out."

"I hope so. But ..." He held his hand out to her. "I'm more interested in this working out."

She followed him up the steps and into the house.

"I thought we had an evening out with a bunch of friends. Now, it seems we're at a loose end. Can you think of anything we might do to fill the evening?" He closed his arms around her with a smile.

"Hmm." She touched the front of his pants. "I can think of a couple of things."

He unfastened her coat and slid his arms inside. "Want to tell me about them?"

She laughed. "I was hoping you might tell me what you'd like to do with me."

He pushed her skirt up around her waist and rocked his hips against her. "I'll do better than that; I'll show you."

# Chapter Seventeen

When Ivan opened his eyes on Saturday morning, he curled his arm around Abbie and hugged her closer to him. She gave a little grunt and snuggled against him but didn't wake. He smiled. He loved it when she stayed over at his place. Of course, he loved what they got to do at night—and during the night, but he thought that maybe he loved this more, this feeling of closeness in the morning. When she'd had to get up and go to work, they'd only had a few minutes, but she was off today. He kissed her hair, breathing in her scent. He could get used to this.

She looked over her shoulder and gave him a sleepy smile. "Is it time to wake up?"

"Not if you don't want to."

She wriggled her ass against him. "I could be persuaded."

He'd thought he should leave her be, but that was an invitation he wasn't about to turn down. He closed his hand around her breast, and the little moan she made had him fully awake. Just as he was thinking about turning her onto her back, she stretched her leg back over his hip.

He lowered his head and nibbled her neck. "You don't want to turn over?"

She shook her head and rocked her hips back against him.

He trailed his fingers down over her ribcage, on down over her stomach, and then slid his hand between her legs. He traced her entrance and then dipped a finger inside. She was already wet for him. He loved that she was hot and wet and ready whenever he wanted her.

"Fingers won't wake me up," she breathed.

He smiled and pulled her leg back, opening her up so that he could enter her.

They both let out a gasp as he thrust his hips. She was so tight, such a perfect fit. He closed his eyes and steadied himself. He could lose it in no time if he didn't take it slow. Abbie wasn't interested in taking it slow. She bounced against him and leaned forward to give him better access. Before he knew it, he was pounding harder and harder with every thrust of his hips, and she was gasping and moaning as she took him deeper and deeper.

He felt as though he was losing himself in her velvety wetness. She closed around him, taking him for all he could give her, and more. His scalp tingled as the pressure built and built inside him. This was too fast, but there was no holding back.

"Oh, oh, oh, Ivan!" She screamed his name as she let herself go, her inner muscles pulsating around him, sending him over the edge to join her. He felt as though he came all the way from his scalp to his toes as he found his release deep inside her. His fingers dug deep into her hips as she pushed back against him. They were flying away together to that place where nothing else existed.

"Abbie!" he gasped. He wanted to tell her that he loved her, but the words wouldn't go as deep as what they were already sharing.

When they lay still, he grazed his teeth over her neck, and she shuddered with an aftershock that took her and then him. He held her tight as it quivered through his whole body.

"Now, that's what I call a good morning," she murmured.

He chuckled. "Me too. But if you would like, we could make that regular morning."

She looked over her shoulder at him. "There's nothing regular about that. I'd call it a Saturday morning special."

He held her gaze. "It could be a regular every morning thing—if you wanted it to be."

She frowned and rolled over to face him. "Every morning?"

He nodded. She knew what he meant; he wasn't going to spell it out.

"What about Mom?"

He raised an eyebrow. "I like your mom. But not in that way."

She laughed and slapped his shoulder. "You know what I mean."

"Of course, I do. But that's not a question for me to answer, is it? I don't know what you want; I don't know what she wants or needs. All I'm doing is letting you know what I want."

She nodded. "I'd like that, too."

He grinned.

"But I don't know, Ivan. She needs me. If I woke up with you every morning, I wouldn't be there for her."

He sighed. "I know. And I would never ever try to come between you and her. If you need to live with her forever, I'll accept that, and I'll be here for whatever you can spare me. But …" He had to say it. "I don't think she needs that, or even wants it." He didn't want to say too much. He would love Abbie to move in with him, but he couldn't push for it.

"I know. I need to get my head around it. Can you be patient with me?"

"Of course, I can. I'm not pushing, I'm just being honest."

"I know. You're the best. I don't deserve—"

He put a finger to her lips. "How many times do I have to tell you?"

She licked his finger and gave him a wicked smile. "Want me to show you what I think you deserve?"

He smiled through pursed lips. She took his finger into her mouth and swirled her tongue over it, making him close his eyes and wonder how he was able to get hard again so soon.

She pulled her head back, sucking the length of his finger until it came out of her mouth with a popping sound.

"Is that what you call a diversion tactic?"

She smiled. "Yeah, are you going to tell me it's not working?"

He closed his eyes and breathed a strangled little *yes* as she kissed her way down his chest.

She looked up at him with wide eyes. "No?"

He shook his head. "In the shower?"

"Oh! Yeah. Good idea."

He took her hand on the way to the bathroom. He loved that she was always so eager to go down on him. But he wanted to clean up before he let her. She was so focused on making sure he got what he wanted, she didn't stop to think what it would mean for herself.

~ ~ ~

"Are you sure you want me to come with you?"

Abbie nodded. "I'm sure. She'll love to see you."

"I'd like to see her, too. I'm not trying to get out of it, but I know she wanted to talk to you."

Abbie made a face. "There'll be plenty of time for that."

"Okay, then."

She knew it was probably unfair of her. Ivan wasn't going to push her to talk to her mom because he didn't want her to think he was trying to come between them. She knew he wasn't, and he never would. But she was putting off having the conversation that her mom kept saying they needed to have.

They'd had a lazy morning at Ivan's place, but she'd told her mom she'd see her at lunchtime, and she wanted him to come with her. She wanted the two of them to get used to being around each other.

"Hi, Mom. I'm home. Ivan's with me," she called when she opened the front door.

"Oh, hey, Abbs. I'll be right down."

Abbie led Ivan through to the kitchen. It smelled amazing, and Abbie had to smile. It looked like her mom had done all her Christmas baking.

"Hey, you two."

"Hi, Nina."

Abbie got the warm and fuzzies when she watched Ivan give her mom a hug and had to stop herself from laughing when her mom waggled her eyebrows at her over his shoulder.

"What are you two up to this weekend?"

"Not much today. I wanted to check how you're doing. Though it looks like you're keeping busy. Did you decide to do your baking in advance for tomorrow? I thought you were baking while Ivan grills, and I sit around eating grapes."

Her mom gave her a wary look. "I am baking in advance, but it's because I can't come."

"You can't? Why not?"

"I'm going up to Stanton Falls with Teresa."

Abbie frowned. That caught her off guard. Her mom hadn't been out and done anything with her old friends since ... well, since her dad had passed. Teresa came over sometimes, but her mom didn't go anywhere. "Why?"

Her mom laughed. "Because I love it up there."

"But Ivan offered ..."

Her mom smiled at Ivan. "And I appreciated the offer very much, but it's not his idea of fun—or yours, for that matter. You two have better things to do."

Abbie scowled. "Yeah. Like making dinner and decorating Ivan's place with you."

Her mom came and put her hand on her arm. "Without me, love. You need to build your foundation with just the two of you, and I need to build my own."

Abbie had to swallow back tears, though where they'd come from, she didn't know.

Her mom turned to Ivan. "I hope you understand?"

Ivan nodded. "I do. I just hope you know that I want you to be part of whatever we build. I think you're feeling that you don't need Abbie's help so much now. But it might take a while before you can both figure out what that needs to look like."

Abbie stared at him through teary eyes.

He gave her an apologetic shrug. "You're both too scared to say that things are changing—that what you each want is changing. But they are. The only way you'll hurt each other is if you don't allow the changes to happen."

Abbie's mom came and put an arm around her shoulders and hugged her to her side. "I can tell you one thing that's changed already, Abbs."

"What's that?"

Her mom chuckled. "You found yourself a good man."

"I did, didn't I?"

To her surprise, Ivan came to them and put his arms around them both. "I can't claim to be an expert at how this family stuff works, but I've waited all my life to be part of one."

"Aww." Her mom dabbed at her eyes and smiled up at him. "Well, you're part of one now. It'll have its ups and downs. I can't promise you it'll always be easy, but I can promise you there'll be cookies."

Ivan laughed. "That's all I need."

~ ~ ~

"Would you rather go back to your mom's place?" They'd come back to Ivan's a little while ago, but Abbie was down, he could tell.

She blew out a sigh. "No. I'm sorry. I don't mean to be a bummer. I'm just … I don't know. I don't even know what's wrong with me. I should be happy, shouldn't I?"

"Well, yeah. I think you should. Your mom's starting to find her own way again—do her own thing. That's good, isn't it?"

"Yeah. It really is." Abbie shook her head. "I know it is, so why do I feel so bummed?"

Ivan put his arm around her shoulders. "Do you think maybe it's because you need her more than she needs you?"

Abbie frowned. "No! I don't need her. I just want to be there for her."

Ivan sucked in a deep breath. "Don't take this wrong. I'm only telling you what I think, and I may be way off. Have you asked yourself why you want it so much? Why it's so important for you to be there for her. Why you were prepared to take your own life down a path that didn't suit you, just because you thought it would make her happy?"

"Because I love her."

"Most people love their parents. They don't adjust the course of their lives for them, though."

Abbie frowned. "Okay. So not just because I love her, but because she's been so lost since Dad died. Because she couldn't manage by herself."

"But now, she can."

Abbie made a face.

"But you still feel you can't live your own life the way you want to because of her. She's made it clear that that's not what she wants or needs. But you still feel the need to do it. Why do you think that is?"

Abbie was quiet for a long time. He felt bad when she looked up at him with tears in her eyes. "Because I'm still trying to make up for what I was like before. I'm still trying to make it up to her and to Dad."

She let out a sob, and he hugged her into his chest. He was glad she could see it. She needed to understand that she was punishing herself in a way. She wanted to make up for the way she used to be. But this wasn't the way to do it.

After a little while, she wiped her sleeve across her eyes and looked up at him. "You're telling me that I can't hold her back because I need to try to make it right."

"I wouldn't put it like that. But I do think that you're holding onto her a little too tight. You don't need to make up for anything. The past is gone. What you need to do now is live your own best life; that'll make her happy."

She nodded. "I think I kind of know that already. It's like I want her to need me because I want to be the daughter I should have been. If she doesn't need me anymore, then I can never be that."

"Abbs." He tucked a strand of hair behind her ear. "You might have made some mistakes when you were younger, but she's always loved you. You don't need to be some other kind of daughter. I told you that first night that we went out. You can't turn yourself into someone else; you just have to try to be the best version of yourself."

"I know. I'm sorry."

He dropped a kiss on her lips. "Would you stop apologizing?"

She sniffed and smiled. "How about you take me to bed and shut me up?"

He got to his feet and pulled her up off the sofa. "If that's what it takes, I suppose I can oblige."

She laughed. "Poor, long-suffering Ivan. He'll sleep with me if he must."

He chuckled as he led her up the stairs. "What can I say? I'm nice like that."

~ ~ ~

Abbie stood back and looked at the tree. "There. I think that does it."

Ivan came and stood behind her and slid his arms around her waist. "I love it."

She turned to look up at him and planted a kiss on his cheek. "I love you."

He pressed a kiss into her hair. "Not as much as I love you."

"Let's not get competitive about it, huh?"

"Okay."

She laughed. "Don't look like that. I'm just saying. Because if we do—I'll win."

He laughed with her. "Well, now that the tree's done, do you think we should start making dinner?"

"Yeah." Abbie checked the clock.

"You think it's too early?"

"No. I'm just wondering what Mom's up to."

He raised an eyebrow at her but didn't say anything.

"I hope she's having a good time. I'm glad she's gone up there with Teresa. She loves Stanton Falls and all the stores. It's just ..." She shrugged. "I know I have to let her get on with it. But if you want to know what it's really all about, part of me feels guilty that I'm finding happiness with you. I feel bad when I think about putting myself first."

"You shouldn't. This is dangerous ground for me because you know what I want. I want you to be with me—and that means being with your mom less. I don't want you to think that I'm being selfish—but in a way, I am."

"No. I get it. You want to be with me. I want to be with you. But I don't want to leave Mom out in the cold."

"We won't."

"I can't. I feel like I have to put her first."

Ivan shook his head. "I can't argue with you—I won't. I think we just need to let things play out as they will." He came to her and put his arms around. "I'm just going to put it out there. So, there's no doubt about it. I want you to move in with me, Abbie. Whenever you're ready."

Her heart pounded in her chest. "I want to. I really do. Just give me some time?"

"Take all the time you need."

"Let's get through Christmas first, can we? I can't imagine leaving her to wake up on her own on Christmas day."

"Of course not. Like I said, I'm not trying to rush you. I just need you to know that's what I want." He planted a kiss on her forehead. "And maybe you can take some time to think about it and admit that it's what you want, too?"

She nodded. She didn't need any time to figure that out. She wanted to live with him. She wanted to be with him forever—whatever that might look like for them. He'd told her that he wasn't going to marry her, and that was fine. If marriage wasn't his thing, she could live with that. "I do want to."

"Let's go make dinner."

She nodded and followed him into the kitchen.

# Chapter Eighteen

Ivan was surprised when he got to work on Monday morning to see that someone had beaten him there. He let himself in and followed the smell of coffee to the break room.

Neil stood there, grinning to himself with a mug of a coffee in his hand.

"Morning."

Neil looked startled. "Oh. Hey. Good morning."

"You look happy," said Ivan as he poured himself a mug.

Neil grinned. "That's because I am. Thanks to you and Abbie."

"Did it work out with you and Merry, then?"

"It couldn't have worked out better. We went to Giuseppe's for dinner, and we talked and laughed, and it was the best date ever."

"That's awesome."

Neil nodded vigorously. "It was amazing. I walked her home, and we kissed goodnight. Then, on Saturday, we met up for lunch and then went back to her place and talked for hours. Yesterday, we went for a drive up to Stanton Falls. Oh, and we ran into Abbie's mom."

Ivan smiled, thrilled at how well things had worked out. "Yeah. She went up there with a friend."

"She said you and Abbie were at home, decorating for Christmas. Are things working out for you, then?"

"They are."

"I'm probably getting ahead of myself here, but I'm curious to see which of us makes it to the altar first."

"The altar?!"

Neil hung his head. "Sorry. I know that's ridiculous. But being with Merry just feels so right. I know she's the one I want to spend my life with—the woman I want to marry." He looked up. "Is that the way you feel about Abbie, or is it more casual for you?"

"It's not casual." Ivan frowned as he thought about it. "Now that you've put it into words, that's exactly how I feel about her. She's the one I want to spend my life with—the woman I want to marry."

Neil grinned. "But you didn't realize it until I said it? Did I help you figure it out? I hope so. I'd like to think that maybe I played a little part in getting the two of you together. You were both so instrumental in helping Merry and me."

Ivan smiled. "Yeah. You can take the credit for it. I didn't think marriage was one of my goals in life, but things change, right? You have to go with the flow."

"You do. Especially when it comes to women. They just come in and turn your world upside down."

"I can vouch for the truth of that."

They both turned to see Mr. D standing in the doorway. He grinned at Ivan. "Did I hear you right? Did you just tell Neil that you're thinking about getting married?"

Ivan sucked in a deep breath and nodded. "Yeah. I didn't know it until just now, but ... yeah." He grinned. "That's what I want."

"And does Abbie know this?"

His smile faded. "She knows I want her to move in with me. But she wants to play it by ear. Get through Christmas first and see how her mom's doing."

Mr. D nodded. "That sounds sensible."

Neil smiled at them both. "I should be getting started."

Mr. D grasped his shoulder as he left. "You're doing a great job, son."

Once he'd gone, Ivan offered Mr. D a coffee, and they took them through to Ivan's office.

"So, she's the one?"

"She is."

"And you want to stay here? Make this your life?"

"I do. I love this place. I love the people. I love my job. I'll always go with you and drive for you whenever you want me to, but I think I've found my calling here."

"I believe you have. I wasn't sure about setting the office up here, but you've done great things for the charities just in the short time we've been here."

"Thanks. I enjoy it, and I'm surprised how easily it comes. I wasn't sure that I was cut out for office work, but this doesn't feel like office work. This is about bringing in donations and making sure the money goes to doing the most good it can for kids who need it."

Mr. D smiled at him. "That's why I knew you'd be able to handle it. You might not have the office experience, but you have the heart. That's the most important. The rest can be learned."

"I hope you know how much I appreciate this."

"I do. And I hope you know how much I value you."

Ivan chuckled. "You've made it pretty clear with everything that you do for me."

"Maybe I haven't made it clear enough—yet."

"What does that mean?"

Mr. D gave him a mysterious smile. "Maybe it doesn't mean anything. Maybe it does."

Ivan laughed. "Well, I'm not going to take up your time trying to figure out your riddles. We're supposed to be going over the New Year's campaigns this morning. Are you ready?"

"Ready and willing. Let's get down to it."

~ ~ ~

Abbie sat scowling at her computer screen. The waiting room was empty. The last patients of the day were in with Michael and Cassie. She'd be able to leave in a little while. But she didn't really even want to. When she left here, she'd have to go home and deal with her mom. And Ivan would be calling, wanting to know if she was going over there tonight. She'd told him she'd call him today, but after the little bombshell her mom had dropped last night, she wanted to wait and call him later.

She forced herself to smile when Mrs. Young came out of Cassie's office. "Goodnight, Abbie. Merry Christmas to you."

"Merry Christmas." Even as she said it, Abbie felt more like Scrooge. If it weren't Christmas, her mom wouldn't have come up with this crazy idea.

"I'm all done, Abbie. I can stay until Michael's finished if you want to leave."

She smiled at Cassie. "That's okay. I don't mind waiting."

"I thought you'd want to get out of here to that sexy man of yours. What happened on Friday? I thought he was coming, and the next thing I heard, you'd left." She grinned. "Did you decide you'd rather be home alone with him instead?"

"No. We were on a mission, playing cupid."

"Oh, for Merry? Did it work out?"

"I hope so. They went for dinner together."

Cassie smiled. "Aww. Look at you matchmaking and everything. You're such a sweetheart."

Abbie made a face. "Ha! I've been called many things, but never a sweetheart. You know what I'm like."

"I do. You're a sweetheart. If you mean that I knew you when you were younger and wilder, then yes, I did, but you've grown up—just like we all have. The Abbie I knew in high school wouldn't have gone out of her way to help two introverts find love—she'd have been more likely to make fun of them. You're not like that anymore. Give yourself some credit."

Abbie stared at her.

"What? It's true. You're a real sweetheart these days, but you still talk about yourself as if you were that girl in high school. She's gone." Cassie's smile faded. "We've all changed since then—some for the better, some for the worse. We're still the same people, though—we just have different priorities now."

They both looked up when Max Douglas came out of Michael's office. "Well, lookit this, two pretty ladies here to bid me goodnight."

Abbie smiled. She loved Mr. Douglas—Gramps, as they'd all called him as kids. "Much as I love to see you, I hope you don't want another appointment?"

"Nope. Michael says he doesn't want me darkening his door again until at least next year. So. I guess I must be doing okay for an old fart."

Abbie laughed. "I guess you must. But in case I don't see you before the new year ..." She came out from behind the desk and gave him a hug. "Merry Christmas."

"Merry Christmas to you, too, young 'un." He nodded at Cassie. "And you. Abbie here's found the spirit of the season. You might want to see if you can find yours."

Cassie gave him a rueful smile. "I'm fine. Merry Christmas, Gramps."

"Aye. Merry Christmas."

They watched him go. Abbie wanted to ask Cassie what he'd meant about her needing to find her Christmas spirit, but she didn't get a chance.

"Well, if you don't want to get out of here, I do. I'll see you tomorrow."

"Okay, see you."

When Abbie got to her car a little while later, she sat behind the wheel for a moment. She should probably call Ivan now to tell him that she wasn't going over to his place tonight.

She dialed his number and waited.

"Hey, sweetie."

"Hi. Sorry I didn't call you today."

"No problem. I figured you were busy. Are you coming over later?"

"No."

"Oh. How come?" She could hear the disappointment in his voice. "Is your mom okay?"

"She thinks so. But I don't."

"What does that mean?"

"You know she went up to Stanton Falls yesterday? Well, one of her old friends runs a store there, and she's short-handed for the Christmas rush. She offered Mom a job, and Mom's packing her things as we speak."

"Packing?"

"Yeah. There's an apartment above the store. She's going to stay there."

"Wow."

"That's a bit milder than what I said."

"What did she say?"

"That she's excited. That this will do her good."

"And you don't believe her?"

Abbie thought about it. "I don't know. Maybe."

"It sounds to me like it could be just what she needs. She wanted to find a job. She loves Christmas, and she loves Stanton Falls. It sounds like she'll be kept busy, and that might not be a bad thing if it helps her get through the holidays."

Abbie sighed.

"Sorry, Abbs, but I have to tell you what I think."

"I know. I'm not mad at you. I'm mad at me, if anything. When she told me last night, I tried to talk her out of it. I should have stopped and thought it through. Everything you just said makes sense, and I know it. But I was looking at it from my point of view, not hers."

"That's only natural."

"But if I keep saying I want to put her first, then I kind of need to listen to what she wants and help her get it, don't I? Not try to make her want what I think she should."

"Yeah."

"Okay. I'm going to head home, then. Help her pack up. Can I call you later?"

"Whenever you like."

"I love you."

"I love you, too."

~ ~ ~

Ivan hung up and went back into the kitchen. He smiled at the sight of the Christmas tree as he passed it. He had to admit it made the house feel like a home. He couldn't help but think that he wanted to share his home with Abbie.

Hopefully, going to Stanton Falls would be a good move for her mom—and maybe it would help Abbie to understand that she didn't need to be there with her in the same way anymore. He turned off the stove. He'd planned to make spaghetti for dinner, but since Abbie wasn't coming, he may as well just grab something from the freezer and nuke it in the microwave.

He pulled his phone out when it rang again, hoping that she'd changed her mind. It wasn't her.

"Hello?"

"Hi, Ivan. It's Nina."

"Oh. Hi."

"Are you coming over to see Abbie tonight?"

"No. I just talked to her. She's on her way home."

Nina blew out a sigh. "Can I tempt you over if I offer you more cookies?"

He laughed. "She wants to spend the evening with you, not me."

"We both know that's not true. She just thinks that's what she supposed to do. But I don't need it."

"She told me about you going to Stanton Falls. She said you're leaving tomorrow. I think she wants you to herself before you go."

"I think she wants to try and talk me out of it, and she's not going to."

Ivan chuckled. "She's only trying to look out for you."

"I know. I just wish she'd listen to me. If you come over, we might be able to convince her between us."

"I'm not sure that's a good idea."

"Please? I'll take all the blame. I won't let her be mad at you."

"I'm not worried about that. I just don't want to get in the middle. You two need to figure this out between you."

"You're probably right. It's not fair of me to ask."

"It's not that." He felt bad. "I just don't think you need anyone else. It should be about the two of you."

She was quiet for a long time, and he hoped she wasn't mad at him or disappointed.

"Maybe I shouldn't say this, but I'm going to. You and Abbie are serious about each other, aren't you?"

"Yes."

"The kind of serious that means you and I are going to get to know each other much better in the years to come."

"I hope so."

"Then, can you see that it's not really about just Abbie and me anymore? It's about the three of us and how we all live our lives going forward. Abbie wants to live with me to keep an eye on me. Tell me if I'm wrong, but you want to live with Abbie."

He didn't see any point denying it. "I do."

She chuckled. "I know in her heart she wants to live with you. And to be honest, I need to live by myself again. I need to figure out what my life's going to be like. And I don't want to be that sad old lady who lives with her daughter."

Ivan chuckled with her. "I don't see you that way."

"That's sweet of you. But that's what I'll become if we don't figure this out. So, please. Come over?"

"Okay."

He still wasn't sure how wise this was when he pulled up outside their house a little while later. At least Abbie was home already. Her car was in the driveway. He didn't like the idea of being there before her. Hopefully, her mom would have warned her he was coming.

When he lifted his hand to knock on the door, he wasn't surprised when Nina opened it with a smile. "Ivan. Come on in."

He gave her a hug and followed her to the kitchen. Abbie was sitting at the counter and slid down to come and peck his cheek. At least, she was smiling.

"Don't look so worried. Mom told me she'd invited you."

He gave her a rueful smile. "I feel like I'm here to referee or something."

Abbie laughed. "No. There's nothing to fight about."

Her mom came and hugged her. "I told Abbie the same thing I told you. I've been wanting to say it for ages, but I couldn't find the right words. They came out easy enough when I told you, so I just repeated them to her."

Ivan nodded, wondering which words she meant.

Abbie leaned against his side. "Since Mom wants to live by herself, and you want to live with me, I'm finally ready to admit that I want to live with you."

A wave of relief swept through him. He raised an eyebrow at her. "Is it really going to be that easy?"

She smiled. "Yes. If I hadn't been such an idiot, it could have been that easy all along. But somehow, between everyone chipping away at me, I've finally gotten it through my thick skull. We all have to live our own lives. We can support each other, but we each have to put ourselves first."

Ivan nodded. "Mind if I ask what your mom said that finally broke through?"

Her mom laughed. "It was easy in the end. Abbie couldn't stand the thought of being selfish. But when I told her I need to be selfish, and I need to figure my own life out, she got it."

Abbie nodded. "When Mom told me that she has to go after what she wants, I totally understood. Then she turned it around on me and asked why I didn't understand it for myself." She shrugged. "And now, I do."

He chuckled. "I'm glad. This is a lot easier than I thought it was going to be."

"Aren't you glad you came now?" asked her mom.

"I am. Especially if I get cookies out of it."

Abbie slapped his arm with a laugh. "You're only here for the cookies."

He put his arm around her shoulders. "Not, just that, but I'm not sure I would have been brave enough to come otherwise."

Her mom smiled at them. "Well, I'll give you both a good dinner this evening, but after that, you'll have to wait until Christmas before I bake you more cookies."

Abbie looked at Ivan. "She's going up there tomorrow and not coming back until Christmas day."

"We can go up on the weekend and visit if you like."

Nina smiled at him. "You can, but only for a quick visit. This is the busiest time of year up there. I expect I'll be rushed off my feet."

"We'll see how it goes," said Abbie. "We'll talk every night on the phone."

Her mom rolled her eyes at Ivan. "I hope you'll be keeping her occupied so she forgets some nights."

His heart started to race as understanding hit him. If her mom wasn't going to be here, there was no reason she couldn't come and stay with him. He looked down at her, and she smiled.

"I don't like the idea of staying here by myself."

He tightened his arm around her shoulders. "So, come home with me."

# Chapter Nineteen

By the time the weekend rolled around, Abbie had already adapted to all the big changes that were happening in her life. Her mom had left for Stanton on Tuesday morning. It had been weird to wave her off, knowing that she was setting off on a new chapter of her own life. It might only be for a few weeks, but Abbie understood now that it was a major turning point in her mom's journey to figuring out what her life was going to be like as a widow.

That evening, she'd gone straight to Ivan's after work. He was so sweet. He'd hung a banner on the Christmas tree that said, "Welcome Home!" And now, just a few days later, it felt like home. It felt like this was where she belonged. Not the house, although she wished that this could be her forever home. It was so beautiful, and she knew it would be even more beautiful in the summer with its view of the lake. But she'd be happy in a shack if she got to live there with Ivan. It was being with him that made her so happy. He was the one who'd helped her get over all the stupid shit she'd had in her head about how she needed to be and how she needed to live her life. Now, he was helping her to see that just being herself was enough. That she could have what she wanted and be happy. She didn't need to feel guilty or to try to live up to some standard that she'd set for herself.

She trotted downstairs while Ivan was still in the shower. He was just like her mom in that he enjoyed his coffee in the morning. She liked to set the pot brewing before he got up and then leave him to enjoy his peace while she showered. She'd been staying with him for less than a week, but they'd already fallen into some comfortable little routines like that. She couldn't remember ever being this happy.

She went to get her phone from the counter when it rang, wondering who could be calling this early on a Saturday morning.

It was her mom.

"Hi. Is everything okay?"

"Everything's wonderful, Abbs. I'm loving this. I'm so busy. The store is slammed the whole time. And the customers are all so nice because they're in the Christmas spirit."

"That's good. I was a bit worried when you didn't answer the phone last night. You didn't even call me back."

"Sorry. We went out for dinner after we closed up."

Abbie frowned. Her Mom's friend Janet owned the store. Abbie had known her for years, but she didn't know who else was working there. "Who's we?"

Her mom laughed. "Janet and me, and Kerry and Jess, who I work with, and a few people from the stores either side of us. Everyone's so friendly up here. The way they go overboard on Christmas, I thought it was just for the tourists, but it seems like the whole community gets involved."

"That sounds nice. So, you're having fun then?"

"I am, Abbs. It's just the right mix of new people and busy work to ensure that I'm either having fun or don't have time to think about the reasons why I shouldn't be."

"There's no reason you shouldn't, Mom."

"I know, but it's hard sometimes. Anyway, I wasn't just checking in. I wanted to talk to you about something, but there never seems to be a good time."

"What's wrong?"

Her Mom laughed. "There's nothing wrong. In fact, I think it's a very good thing. Janet has asked me if I want to stay on after the holidays."

"Oh!" Abbie wanted to ask all kinds of questions, but she'd finally learned that what she needed to do was listen to what her mom thought—and what she wanted—and do her best to support her in whatever that might be.

"Yes. Jess is ready to retire, and they're going to need to hire someone full time. I fit in with everyone. We all get along. It makes sense. But would you mind?"

"Of course not. All I ever wanted was for you to be happy, Mom. I wasn't trying to control you. I just ..."

"I never thought you were, Abbs. I care about what you think. I don't want you to feel like you came to Summer Lake, and then I moved away and abandoned you."

"No. It's not far. We can see each other whenever we want. If it's going to make you happy, I can keep an eye on the house for you."

Her mom was quiet for a long moment. "I was thinking it might be time to sell the house."

"Oh." Abbie sucked in a deep breath. She was doing her best to be supportive here, but that was a tough one.

"Not straight away, and maybe not at all, but it might be for the best. What do you think?"

"I don't know what to think, Mom. But you don't need to decide right now, do you?"

"No. I just wanted to let you know what I'm thinking. Anyway, how's Ivan? How are the two of you getting along?"

"He's wonderful, Mom. I love him."

"Aww. And he loves you, too."

"He does." Abbie looked up as he came down the stairs and headed straight for the coffee. He gave her an inquiring look. "It's Mom."

"Oh. Say hi for me. Is she coming for Christmas?"

Abbie spoke back into her phone. "He's up. He's asking if you're coming for Christmas."

Her mom laughed. "Tell him I said yes, but he can call and tell me if he'd rather I didn't."

Abbie laughed. "I know you two and your calls behind my back, but you won't need to sneak around on this one. He's hoping you'll come."

"In that case, yes. I'll be there. But I won't arrive until mid-morning. I'm working Christmas eve, and I won't drive back to the lake in the dark."

"Okay. Well, there's time to figure out what we're doing."

"There is, but I don't have any time left to chat with you. I need to get ready for work."

"Oh." Abbie looked at the clock. "I do, too. It's my Saturday on."

"Love you, Abbs. I'll talk to you soon."

"Love you, Mom. Bye."

Ivan came to her and dropped a kiss on her lips. "Is she okay?"

"She sounds great. She was out last night. She's enjoying herself and …" She sucked in a deep breath. "Janet's asked her if she wants to stay on after the holidays. She's talking about moving up there and selling the house."

"Wow! How do you feel about that?"

She shrugged. "I don't know. But … yeah, I do. I think as long as it makes her happy, then I'm happy."

He slid his arms around her waist. "That's all it's about, you know. Being happy."

"I know."

"I want to make you happy, Abbie."

"You do."

"You make me happy, too. So happy that I don't want this to ever end. I didn't want to ask if you were going to stay here once your mom came back, but if she's not coming back …" He raised an eyebrow. "Even if she does, will you stay, live with me, make this permanent?"

She nodded happily. "I will."

He dropped his head and kissed her. She clung to him, feeling as though she was finally getting it right. At first, she'd thought Ivan was the wrong kind of guy. Now she understood that he was the perfect guy for her.

When he lifted his head, he smiled. "How would you feel about having some people over for dinner?"

"Tonight?"

"No." He laughed. "I wouldn't land it on you like that. Maybe next Friday? It's the last weekend before Christmas. I said that we'd have dinner with Chris and Seymour. I thought maybe we could invite them over, but then there's Merry and Neil—by the sounds of it, they're spending every waking minute together. Then I thought that's my work people, maybe you'd want to invite yours, too, and Logan and Roxy and the gang."

"That's a lot of dinner."

"Okay. So how about just drinks and snacks? We could even call it our official house-warming party."

"Okay. Let's do it. As long as I don't have to make dinner, I'd love to."

~ ~ ~

Ivan looked around the house. He finally understood what everyone had been talking about when they said he needed to put his mark on the place. It looked so much different than it had just a couple of months ago. Abbie had said it looked like it had been staged ready to sell. Now, it looked like a home. His and Abbie's home. The tree twinkled in the corner, but it wasn't just the Christmas decorations. There were more paintings, too. And a lamp that she'd brought him. She'd found his box of books in the closet, and they'd spent an evening filling the bookshelves with them; it still surprised him how much of a difference that made.

Abbie came and stood behind him and slipped her arms around his waist. "Are you doing okay?"

"I'm great. I'm just thinking how you've made this place into a home."

She looked around. "I guess we have, haven't we? And tonight, we welcome our friends into our home." She grinned. "I'm looking forward to it."

"Me too. Did I tell you that Neil said he and Merry will be here early?"

Abbie laughed. "You didn't, but it doesn't surprise me. They probably want to get in and out before everyone else arrives."

"Yep, that's what he said."

"I can't believe that I actually went on a date with him—that I thought I could possibly have a future with him."

Ivan scowled. "I don't like to be reminded of that."

She laughed and pushed at his arm. "What, that I was so stupid?"

"No." He curled his arm around her and pulled her against him. "That there was a time that you went on dates with other guys. No more dating for you, lady—ever."

Her eyes widened as she looked up into his.

For a moment, he thought she was mad, that she might say he didn't get to tell her what she could do.

Instead, she relaxed against him. "I hope I never go on another date in my life—with anyone who isn't you."

He had to swallow the lump that formed in his throat. He kind of knew she felt that way, but he hadn't been one hundred percent sure until now. "I'll do my best to make sure you never have to."

He lowered his lips to hers but stopped when the doorbell rang.

She pecked him and then pulled away. "We'd better let them in."

They were right about Neil and Merry. They stayed less than half an hour, and when people started arriving, they only chatted with Mr. D and Chris for a couple of minutes before making their excuses and leaving.

Ivan smiled as he watched Chris and Abbie disappear into the kitchen. He had a lot of respect for Chris, and he was glad that Abbie knew and liked her, too.

"If you'd told me a year ago when we were in Montana that this is where we'd be today, I would have told you that you were crazy."

Ivan turned to see Mr. D standing beside him.

"I wouldn't have believed it myself."

Mr. D smiled. "It's amazing how much can change in twelve months. What if I asked you to predict where we'll be this time next year?"

Ivan thought about it. "Hmm. I'd say that you and Chris will be married. I reckon you might even have bought a house here. You say you love her place, but I still think you'd be happier in a house like this. It feels weird that I live here while you live with her."

Mr. D laughed. "You might be right on that one. I do love her house, but ever since I got interested in cooking, I'd love a bigger kitchen, if nothing else."

"You could take over this place if you want." Ivan didn't like the idea of leaving the first house he'd ever come to think of as home, but Mr. D was the one paying for it, and it was more his style.

"No way. This is your place."

"It's not, though, is it?"

Mr. D gave him an odd look. "It is. You've made it your home. You and Abbie. This is where you're starting your life together." He smiled. "You didn't finish your prediction. You said I'd be married this time next year—will you?"

Ivan smiled. "I hope so. I plan to be engaged, but the married part is dependent on a wedding—and that will depend on Abbie and what she wants to do."

Mr. D smiled. "You should have a big wedding, whatever she wants."

"I'll do my best."

"Well, I guess we'll have to check in this time next year and see how we each fared. For now, I'm going to have a word with Jack. I didn't know you'd invited him."

"We invited everyone. It's kind of our house-warming party. Even though I've been here a while, Abbie's agreed to live with me now, so …" He shrugged.

Mr. D gave him that weird smile again before he went to talk to Jack.

Logan came and slung an arm around his shoulders. "Damn, bud. I knew you lived in a big fancy house, but this place is something else."

"Thanks. I like it. It's not as though it's mine, though. It comes with the job."

"I'd take it any way it comes. It's awesome. I told you you'd be one of the couples before long, and look at you, doing it in style. You've got the lovely Abbie tamed, and the two of you are setting up home together in this place. You'll be in magazines next—beautiful people and their beautiful homes."

Ivan laughed. "I don't know about that, but I can tell you, I'm happy."

"And you're happy to stay here?"

Ivan gave him a puzzled look, and then he remembered what Logan had said about Abbie never leaving her mom. "I am. I love this town. But if you're thinking about Abbie's mom, that's all changed. She's got a job in Stanton Falls. She's talking about moving there permanently."

"Wow."

Roxy appeared at Logan's side. "Did I hear mention of Stanton Falls? Are we going up there? We never did make that group trip happen. We should all go in the new year sometime."

"That wasn't what we were talking about," said Logan. "But yeah, we should see who's up for it. It'd be a fun trip if a bunch of us go."

Ivan smiled. Their group of friends had talked about going up to Stanton Falls a while back, but it hadn't come off. He hadn't been keen on the idea at the time. Now, with Abbie, it'd be fun.

~ ~ ~

It was midnight before the last people left. Abbie was exhausted. She hadn't expected it to go this late, but everyone had been having a good time. And she'd enjoyed herself.

Ivan came and put his arms around her. "I think we can say it was a success."

She smiled and rested her head against his shoulder. "I think we can. It was great. Is it weird that it feels like we're official now? That somehow having this party was some kind of landmark—for us and for all our friends."

His lips quirked up in the hint of a smile.

"What? Do you think I'm goofy for seeing it that way?"

"No. I'm smiling because I'm proud of myself."

"Why?"

"Because I hoped it'd make you feel that way. Do you seriously think that I'm the kind of guy who sees himself as the host?"

"No. Now you come to mention it, I don't. So, why did you come up with this?"

"For you, for us." He held her closer. "You want to feel like you're more respectable now, part of the community, not on the edges." He planted a kiss on her forehead. "You thought you'd be getting a life like that if you married an accountant." He smiled at her. "You wouldn't have gotten it with Neil."

She laughed. "No, I wouldn't. But, Ivan, I don't need it either. I don't care about that stuff."

"I know. I just wanted to show you that with me, you can have it if you want it. You can have whatever is in my power to give you. That's how much I love you."

"Aww. I love you, too. I ..." She made herself stop. She'd been about to say that she didn't deserve him, but she knew what he'd say to that, and more importantly, she knew it wasn't true anymore.

# Chapter Twenty

On Christmas morning, Ivan opened his eyes and smiled. Today was the day. He didn't usually make much of an effort for Christmas. It was just another day for him. Not this year, though, and he hoped that for the rest of his life, Christmas would have a new meaning for him, a very special, very important one.

He put his arm around Abbie and pulled her closer. She gave him a sleepy smile. "Mm. Are you going to give me my Christmas present right now?" She wiggled her ass against him.

Damn, he wanted her. And there was no reason not to. "Is this what you want for Christmas?" he asked as he pressed his cock between her legs.

"Mm." She rolled onto her back and held her arms up to him. "Yes, please."

Her hands roved over his back and shoulders as he kissed her. She started out sleepy and slow, but before long, she was spreading her legs wider, rocking her hips against him and grasping his ass. "I want you, Ivan."

"I'm all yours," he breathed against her neck.

Her fingers closed around him, and he closed his eyes as she guided him inside her. He tried to take it slow; he liked the idea of long, slow lovemaking on Christmas morning. Abbie had other ideas.

She raked her fingers down his back and then dug her nails into his ass, urging him to move faster, harder, to give her more and more until all his pent-up desire found its release inside her. She gasped his name as she came with him, milking him for all he had to give as they soared away together. When he finally slumped down on her shoulder, she nibbled his ear. "I love you, Ivan."

"I love you more, Abbs."

It was ten o'clock by the time they made breakfast. They'd stayed in bed awhile, then had coffee and opened presents and showered. It was the most perfect Christmas day Ivan had ever had—and the best part was still to come.

She poured a glass of orange juice and set it down on the counter in front of him. "I had a text from Mom; she said she should be here at noon."

"That's good, and it's warm out there. The roads should be clear for her."

"Yeah. I checked the forecast this morning. There's no frost."

He smiled. He had a feeling that they would always look out for her mom as if they were the parents. He didn't mind that one bit. He liked her a lot. He could see himself growing to love her. She'd invited him to be a part of their family early on. A few days ago, she'd happily told him that she would love for him to make that official. Now all he needed to do was to wait for her to get here so he could. She'd told him that she didn't need to be there, but he wanted to include her.

Abbie ran out onto the driveway when her mom pulled up and wrapped her in a hug. "Merry Christmas."

"Merry Christmas to you, too."

Abbie stood back and looked at her. "Wow! You look amazing. Did you get your hair done?"

"I did. Do you like it?"

"I love it. But come on in. It's freezing out here."

"Give me a minute. Let me bring your presents in."

Abbie helped her bring her bags up to the house and led her through to the kitchen, where Ivan was stirring a pot on the stove.

"Hey." He came and gave her mom a hug. "Merry Christmas."

She grinned at him. "Merry Christmas to you, too. I'm so excited. I didn't think I'd enjoy this Christmas, but now—" She stopped short and shot a look at Abbie that she didn't understand.

"Now, what?"

To her surprise, both her mom and Ivan looked guilty as hell.

"What is it? Will one of you tell me what's going on?"

Her mom looked at Ivan. "Maybe you should."

For a moment, she was scared. Ivan looked panicked. He shoved his hands in his pockets and then relaxed.

"What is it?"

He came and took her hand and led her through to the living room. Her mom followed.

"It's nothing bad, Abbie. Don't look like that. It's something good—at least, I hope you'll think so."

She gave him a puzzled look. They both seemed so happy, it didn't feel like something awful was about to happen.

"Okay." She smiled. "Why don't you just tell me, and I can decide for myself?"

"Okay!" He took a deep breath and dropped down on one knee in front of her. "I know the first night we went out I told you I wasn't going to marry you. Well, I'm hoping I was wrong."

Her heart pounded in her chest as she stared down at him.

"I got you this." He held up a beautiful diamond ring. "In case you want to make this official. What I'm trying to say here is, I love you, Abbie. I want to spend the rest of my days with you. Will you marry me?"

She nodded happily as tears ran down her cheeks. "Yes! Oh, God, yes!"

He got up and slid the ring on her finger, then closed his arms around her and kissed her. When they finally came up for air, she remembered that her mom was there when she threw her arms around them.

"I'm so happy for you guys."

The three of them hugged for a long moment, and Abbie felt as though they were cementing the foundation of their new little family unit.

Her mom stepped back and smiled. "I have to tell you that I do plan to move to Stanton, but I've been thinking. If you want the house, you can have it."

Abbie smiled and thanked her, but she didn't love the idea. She could tell that Ivan didn't either. She didn't want to start her married life in her childhood home. And besides, they both loved this place so much.

Ivan went and pulled a bottle of champagne from the fridge and popped it open. Abbie laughed. "I wondered what that was for."

They all turned at the sound of the doorbell, and Ivan went to see who it was. Abbie was surprised to see Seymour Davenport out there. She expected Ivan to bring him in, but instead, he stepped outside with him and closed the door.

Her mom came and hugged her. "I'm so happy for you, Abbs. He's a wonderful man. I know you'll be happy together. Now. Let me see that ring."

Abbie held her hand up, and they both admired the gorgeous ring that her gorgeous man had given her. Her fiancé. She tried out the word and discovered that she loved it. But not as much as she loved him.

She glanced at the door, hoping that everything was okay. She'd have to go and check in a minute.

When he came back in, she went to him; he looked as though he had tears in his eyes. "What is it?"

He smiled. "Sorry. I … I'm … kind of blown away right now."

"Is Seymour okay?"

Ivan half laughed, half hiccupped, as though he was trying not to cry.

"Ivan, tell me!"

He swiped his sleeve over his eyes. "Everything's fine. I'm being a soft ass. These are happy tears, not sad ones. See this?" He held up an envelope.

"What is it?"

"Mr. D. He knew what I was planning to do today, and he wanted to give me a little Christmas gift to help get us started on married life. This …" He waved the envelope. "This is the deed to this house. That's my Christmas present."

Abbie shook her head in disbelief. "He gave you the house?"

Ivan nodded and wrapped his arms around her. "He sure did. I wasn't sure that I had enough to offer you, Abbie. All I had was a heart full of love and the determination to make our life together good." He smiled. "Now, I can give us a home, too."

Abbie snuggled against his chest. "I don't need you to give me anything other than yourself and your love. But if you want to love me here in your amazing house, I'm not going to complain."

"It's not my amazing house, Abbie. It's our home." He dropped a kiss on her lips. "We've come a long way since the

SJ McCoy

day I told you that I'd be there for you if ever you needed a friend to help you chase the blues away, huh?"

She smiled up at him. "We have. You chased them away yourself just by being you."

It was true. She knew how lucky she was, not just that she'd found him, but that he'd been prepared to wait for her and love her through until she saw his worth and finally learned her own. She wasn't perfect, she never would be, but she'd come a long way. And she planned to spend the rest of her days being the best version of herself that she could be, for him;

;

# A Note from SJ

I hope you enjoyed Ivan and Abbie's story. Please let your friends know about the books if you feel they would enjoy them as well. It would be wonderful if you would leave me a review, I'd very much appreciate it.

Check out the "Also By" page to see if any of my other series appeal to you – I have a couple of ebook freebie series starters, too, so you can take them for a test drive.

There are a few options to keep up with me and my imaginary friends:

The best way is to Sign up for my Newsletter at my website www.SJMcCoy.com. Don't worry I won't bombard you! I'll let you know about upcoming releases, share a sneak peek or two and keep you in the loop for a couple of fun giveaways I have coming up :0)

You can join my readers group to chat about the books or like my Facebook Page www.facebook.com/authorsjmccoy
I occasionally attempt to say something in 140 characters or less(!) on Twitter

And I'm in the process of building a shiny new website at www.SJMcCoy.com

I love to hear from readers, so feel free to email me at SJ@SJMcCoy.com if you'd like. I'm better at that! :0)

I hope our paths will cross again soon. Until then, take care, and thanks for your support—you are the reason I write!

Love

SJ

# PS Project Semicolon

You may have noticed that the final sentence of the story closed with a semi-colon. It isn't a typo. <u>Project Semi Colon</u> is a non-profit movement dedicated to presenting hope and love to those who are struggling with depression, suicide, addiction and self-injury. Project Semicolon exists to encourage, love and inspire. It's a movement I support with all my heart.

*"A semicolon represents a sentence the author could have ended, but chose not to. The sentence is your life and the author is you."* - Project Semicolon

This author started writing after her son was killed in a car crash. At the time I wanted my own story to be over, instead I chose to honour a promise to my son to write my 'silly stories' someday. I chose to escape into my fictional world. I know for many who struggle with depression, suicide can appear to be the only escape. The semicolon has become a symbol of support, and hopefully a reminder – Your story isn't over yet

# Also by SJ McCoy

**Summer Lake Silver**
Clay and Marianne in Like Some Old Country Song
Seymour and Chris in A Dream Too Far

**Summer Lake Seasons**
Angel and Luke in Take These Broken Wings
Zack and Maria in Too Much Love to Hide

**Summer Lake Series**
Love Like You've Never Been Hurt (FREE in ebook form)
Work Like You Don't Need the Money
Dance Like Nobody's Watching
Fly Like You've Never Been Grounded
Laugh Like You've Never Cried
Sing Like Nobody's Listening
Smile Like You Mean It
The Wedding Dance
Chasing Tomorrow
Dream Like Nothing's Impossible
Ride Like You've Never Fallen
Live Like There's No Tomorrow
The Wedding Flight

**Remington Ranch Series**
Mason (FREE in ebook form) and also available as Audio
Shane
Carter
Beau
Four Weddings and a Vendetta

## A Chance and a Hope
Chance is a guy with a whole lot of story to tell. He's part of the fabric of both Summer Lake and Remington Ranch. He needed three whole books to tell his own story.

Chance Encounter
Finding Hope
Give Hope a Chance

## Love in Nashville
Autumn and Matt in Bring on the Night

## The Davenports
Oscar
TJ
Reid

## The Hamiltons
Cameron and Piper in Red wine and Roses
Chelsea and Grant in Champagne and Daisies
Mary Ellen and Antonio in Marsala and Magnolias
Marcos and Molly in Prosecco and Peonies
## Coming Next
Grady

# About the Author

I'm SJ, a coffee addict, lover of chocolate and drinker of good red wines. I'm a lost soul and a hopeless romantic. Reading and writing are necessary parts of who I am. Though perhaps not as necessary as coffee! I can drink coffee without writing, but I can't write without coffee.

I grew up loving romance novels, my first boyfriends were book boyfriends, but life intervened, as it tends to do, and I wandered down the paths of non-fiction for many years. My life changed completely a few years ago and I returned to Romance to find my escape.

I write 'Sweet n Steamy' stories because to me there is enough angst and darkness in real life. My favorite romances are happy escapes with a focus on fun, friendships and happily-ever-afters, just like the ones I write.

These days I live in beautiful Montana, the last best place. If I'm not reading or writing, you'll find me just down the road in the park - Yellowstone. I have deer, eagles and the occasional bear for company, and I like it that way :0)